Praise for

She Rides Shotgun

"Fascinating . . . tightly written. . . . Readers will find this book hard—hard to put down."　　　　　　　　　　　　—*St. Louis Post-Dispatch*

"Polly will charm readers instantly. She's fresh and winning. . . . A gritty, dark thriller packed with action."　　—*Dallas Morning News*

"One of the most striking debuts I have read this year. Visceral, violent and utterly compelling, it nevertheless shines with humanity."

—*Daily Mail* (UK)

"A thrill-a-minute read. . . . This debut is gutsy, like grab-you-by-the-throat thrillers by Tom Franklin, Wiley Cash and Ron Rash. . . . Tension mounts as the final scenes play out. You'll read this one quickly and then be sorry it's over."　　　　—*Washington Missourian*

"An impeccable crime novel with a giant heart, massive doses of hatred, vengeance, pain, and violence, and some of the sharpest, tightest prose you'll encounter in 2017."　　　　　　　　—*LitReactor*

"A *True Grit* sort of saga, but on hot-wired horsepower instead of horseback. With Harper's storytelling chops, it's a rolling hell-bent adventure with all the snappy dialogue and action of the best noir fiction."　　　　　　　　　　　　　　　—*Shelf Awareness*

"Urgent and beautiful. The writing is as sharp as broken glass but it's the characters who will stay with you, bloody hearts pinned on their sleeves and struggling for redemption and toward each other."

—Lauren Beukes, author of *The Shining Girls*

"In Polly McClusky, the eleven-year-old girl at the heart of his darkly irresistible debut novel *She Rides Shotgun*, Jordan Harper gives us a hero for our times. With shades of Mattie Ross but an intelligence and fervor all her own, she is unforgettable."

—Megan Abbott, author of *You Will Know Me*

"Confident, brutal, but always human, Jordan Harper's *She Rides Shotgun* is a violent parable of family and sacrifice. The best debut novel that I've read this year."

—Johnny Shaw, Anthony Award–winning author of *Big Maria*

"*She Rides Shotgun* has more kicks than any crime fiction out there, sure, but it's also got a heart that'll keep you up nights, slapping your head and pacing. Don't try to tell me this is a debut novel; I won't hear anything but Jordan Harper's a master."

—Benjamin Whitmer, author of *Cry Father*

"From its bravura prologue to its immensely satisfying ending, this first novel comes out with guns blazing and shoots the chambers dry."

—*Booklist* (starred review)

"The characters' loyalty, love, and struggle for redemption grip the reader and don't let go." —*Kirkus Reviews* (starred review)

"Visceral. . . . Expert pacing and well-developed characters lift this above the thriller pack." —*Publishers Weekly* (starred review)

"An exquisitely violent father-daughter story, burns bright and fast. I kept waiting for the inevitable slow-down, but it never came. An extremely impressive debut."

—Peter Swanson, author of *The Kind Worth Killing*

"Quite simply one of the best debuts I've ever read. Beautifully and lyrically written, it's like a perfect song you hear for the first time and feel like you've always known it. It's an instant classic and if I read a better novel this year, I will be amazed." —Simon Toyne, author of *Sanctus*

"A wholly original take on the relationship between fathers and daughters, this fast-paced and gritty page-turner explores the ways in which love can both brutalize and redeem us. I cared about these characters and imagine other readers will be just as drawn to Nate and Polly." —Amy Engel, author of *The Roanoke Girls*

SHE RIDES SHOTGUN

ALSO BY JORDAN HARPER

LOVE AND OTHER WOUNDS: STORIES

SHE RIDES SHOTGUN

JORDAN HARPER

ecco

An Imprint of HarperCollinsPublishers

SHE RIDES SHOTGUN. Copyright © 2017 by Jordan Harper. All rights reserved. Printed in the United States of America. No part of this book may be used or reproduced in any manner whatsoever without written permission except in the case of brief quotations embodied in critical articles and reviews. For information, address HarperCollins Publishers, 195 Broadway, New York, NY 10007.

HarperCollins books may be purchased for educational, business, or sales promotional use. For information, please email the Special Markets Department at SPsales@harpercollins.com.

FIRST ECCO PAPERBACK EDITION PUBLISHED 2018.

A hardcover edition of this book was first published in 2017 by Ecco, an imprint of HarperCollins Publishers.

Designed by Suet Yee Chong

Title page photography © Olaf Naami / Shutterstock, Inc.

Library of Congress Cataloging-in-Publication Data has been applied for.

ISBN 978-0-06-239441-5

18 19 20 21 22   LSC   10 9 8 7 6 5 4 3 2 1

IN MEMORY OF KENNETH CROSSWHITE

The road was so dimly lighted;
There were no highway signs to guide;
But they made up their minds
If all roads were blind
They wouldn't give up till they died.

—Bonnie Parker, *written on the run*

0

CRAZY CRAIG

—

PELICAN BAY

His skin told his history in tattoos and knife scars. He lived in a room with no night. And he was to his own mind a god.

Crazy Craig Hollington, Pelican Bay lifer, president of the prison gang known as Aryan Steel, which made him the president of all the dirty whiteboys in California, lived his life in a Supermax cell where the lights were on twenty-four hours a day. He couldn't own anything firmer than a Q-tip. They rolled his shower stall to the door of his cell twice a week to keep him from the other prisoners. But he was a god made of other men.

He had men for a mouth. That's how the death warrants left Supermax. A bent guard on Aryan Steel's payroll brought the warrants from Crazy Craig to the plugged-in whiteboys in gen pop.

He had men for blood. They moved Crazy Craig's death warrants around the prison on kites, pieces of paper swung on a string from cell to cell. "To all solid soldiers on the block or on the street," the warrants began. They were signed with the motto "steel forever, forever steel." The words in between described a vendetta. The warrants named the three condemned: A man. A woman. A child. The warrants spelled out specific acts of bloodshed. The warrants were Defcon Old Testament.

He had men for feet. The cons sent the warrants out into the world. They sent them out in pigpen ciphers worked into letters home. As thumbtack braille punched through deposition paperwork. As dried piss painted onto the backs of envelopes, invisible until the paper was held to fire. They sent them out in the visiting room, a featherwood passing her man a balloon of dope in a kiss, him passing her back the death warrants in a whisper. The warrants spread through California wherever peckerwood gangsters and white trash hustlers made camp. They read them in Slabtown and Sun Valley and Fontucky. The warrants went out through Aryan Steel associates and wannabes. They moved through the memberships of shitkicker gangs who paid allegiance to the Steel. Peckerwood Nation. The Nazi Dope Boys. The Blood Skins. Odin's Bastards.

He had men for eyes. A couple of skinheads in Huntington Beach—three-day strangers from sleep on a crank binge—put together wanted posters. They put the pictures to the death warrants, made them official. They quoted the death warrants verbatim. They tacked on rumors. They pulled pictures off the Internet. The man's mug shot. The woman and child, pictured together. The posters got passed around. People memorized the facts, the words, the faces.

He had men for hands. It only took a few days all told before the posters came to a man with a throat-cut tattoo and fuck-you-money ambitions. Addresses were compiled. Plans made. Weapons secured. Blood pacts sealed.

His will be done.

PART I

THE GIRL FROM VENUS

—

THE INLAND EMPIRE

1

POLLY

—

FONTANA

She wore a loser's slumped shoulders and hid her face with her hair, but the girl had gunfighter eyes.

Gunfighter eyes just like her dad, her mom would tell her, usually after a few whiskey pops when Mom could talk about her ex-husband without the anger she carried for him poisoning her. She'd crunch ice and tell Polly about that special type of pale blue eyes. How Wild Bill Hickok and Jesse James and fighter pilots all had them. How sniper schools hunted for recruits with those washed-out blues. Polly didn't tell her mother what she really thought, but if she had she would have said all that stuff about gunfighter eyes sounded like bullcrap. Polly couldn't have gunfighter eyes because she wasn't a gunfighter. Polly did no violence, not to anything but the skin around her fingernails and the flesh of her lips, both of which she chewed raw.

So Polly didn't think much about gunfighter eyes. At least she didn't until the day she walked out the front door of Fontana Middle School and stood there staring into her father's eyes.

Gunfighter eyes, no lie. They were faded blue just like her own, but with something under the surface of them that made Polly's heart beat in her neck. Later on she learned that eyes don't only reflect what they're seeing. They also reflect what they've already seen.

Polly had not seen her dad in nearly half her eleven years, but she knew him without doubt. And seeing him standing there she knew something else too. He must have broke out. Her dad was a bad guy and a robber and he was supposed to be in jail. He liked being a bad guy more than he'd liked being a husband or a father, that's what her mom said. Polly knew sometimes he'd sent letters, but her mom never let her read them, and he'd quit a few years ago anyway. She knew that to have a bad guy for a father was pretty much the same thing as not having one at all. Especially when they're in jail. She'd heard her mom say that he still had at least four more years left before they'd even think of letting him go, and that was if he had good behavior, a thing her mom doubted very much that Nate McClusky could ever have.

So if he was standing here and not in Susanville, he must have broke out. Polly wondered if she should run, or maybe if she ought to yell for an adult, one of the other parents or a teacher. But she didn't do any of those things. She just stood there letting the fear freeze her.

Maybe she wouldn't have to scream and yell for help. Any grown-up who looked had to see there was something wrong going on. Her dad didn't look like he belonged there with the other parents, who all had soft parent bodies and soft parent eyes. He had a face carved out of pebbled rock and tattoos all over, the kind of stuff the boys in her class drew on the backs of their notebooks, dragons and eagles and men with axes. His muscles seemed so big and sharply drawn it was like he was missing his skin, like the tattoos were inked right into the muscle. His hair, which in pictures was the same dirty blond as her own, had been shaved clean away. There was a look on his face, one Polly had never seen on it before in the couple of pictures of him she'd found over the years or her own blurred memories. She couldn't quite figure out what that look meant, but whatever it was it made her feel even worse.

It was a hot day with a dirty sky, and the kids moved quickly to their parents' air-conditioned cars. They ignored her the way lions ignore gazelles when they already have blood on their chops. Even in this crazy second, with her escaped convict dad standing over her like something from a hide-your-eyes movie, Polly felt a loser's blessed relief at being passed by.

Madison Cartwright, who'd been the first to call her Polly Pudding-Ass back in the fourth grade, bumped into her, too busy on her phone to see where she was going. Madison always had new clothes and she already had boobs and she moved through life easy, as if she was on the moon. Her glare made Polly feel hot, like her eyes shot Superman beams. Madison opened her mouth to say something knifelike. Then she saw Polly's dad standing there, all muscles and dragons and gunfighter eyes. She turned and walked away fast with her mouth hanging open, so ridiculous that Polly would have laughed if she wasn't so close to tears.

So it was just Polly and her dad standing there with nothing but dirty air and silence between them, like a high noon standoff in one of those cowboy movies her stepdad liked.

"Polly," her dad said, his voice scratchy as wool. "You know me? Know who I am?"

Her tongue felt too thick for talking, so she just nodded like *yes*. Hardly even thinking, she reached behind herself to where the bear's head poked out of her backpack and gave his ear a squeeze. It helped, like it always did. She held down the urge to take the bear out and press him to her chest.

"Listen close," her dad said. "You're coming with me. Right now, no time for fuss."

He turned and walked toward the street. Her brain told her not to follow him. Her brain said *run inside and find Mr. Richardson*. It told her to scream *help help help*.

But she didn't do any of it. Even though she wanted to run with everything she had, she followed. The urge to run, the urge to scream for help, she shoved them down where she shoved down everything else. What else could she ever do?

HE LED HER to an old man of a car with its windows all rolled down. She got in, her backpack between her knees so that the bear looked up at her with his single scratched black eye.

The silver cap where the key should have gone into the neck of the steering wheel was missing. Metal and wires poked out from the hole that sat there in its place. Her dad fished under the seat and brought out a long dull screwdriver. He jammed it into the hole and twisted. The car *coughed*. It didn't start.

Polly put together the missing key and how her dad was a bad guy, and she understood that she was sitting in a stolen car. She looked out the window back at the school like maybe somehow she'd see real-life Polly still standing there under the dirty sky.

Polly unzipped her backpack enough to pull the bear loose. He stood a foot tall, brown with white on his paws, ears, and snout, although the white parts weren't really white anymore. They were the color of the manila paper Polly used in art class. One of his black glass eyes was missing, leaving only a dry patch of glue like glaucoma. She moved the bear with practiced hands so he stood on her lap and looked around. She had practiced with him for hours and hours so he moved with a liquid sort of grace, like a true and living thing.

"Shoot, girl," her mom had said once, "some days I feel like I know what that stuffed bear is thinking a hell of a lot more than I know what *you're* thinking."

Hearing Mom in her head made Polly now wonder where she was. Why she would let this happen to Polly.

"Little old for teddy bears, ain't you?" her dad asked.

The bear shook his head like *no*. Her dad eyed Polly that way people did when she moved the bear like he was alive. The look was a question. The question was *are you nutso?*

Polly didn't think she was nutso. She knew she was too old for teddy bears. She knew the bear wasn't alive. She knew he was only stuffing and fuzz. She just didn't care.

She probably was nutso.

She watched the bear dance in her hands until she was calm enough, focused enough to ask the question she'd wanted to ask since she first saw her dad.

"Did you break out?"

Her dad puffed air out his nose, sort of a second cousin to a laugh.

"Nope. Got sprung on some lawyer shit."

Polly didn't know what that meant, which made everything worse. A breakout at least was a thing her brain could label and understand. She couldn't make any sense of *lawyer shit*.

He got the engine to come to life. But before he could pull out he caught something in the rearview mirror that made him sit straight and tall in his seat. Polly turned in her seat to see what he was looking at. A police car moved past them school-zone slow.

Polly had a feeling she'd never had before, like the whole world and everything in it was nothing but a pane of glass that could shatter at any second.

The cop car passed out of sight. Her dad said something to himself. It sounded to Polly like he said *goddamn zombie walking*, but why would anybody ever say that?

The cop was gone, but that feeling that the whole world that had felt so solid minutes before was only glass, it didn't leave Polly. Not then, and not ever.

Her dad pulled into traffic. Polly caught a shimmer of herself in the sideview mirror and knew what the look on her dad's face that she'd never seen before had been. A look that looked so at home on Polly's face and so wrong on the face of her father.

The look on his face was fear.

2

POLLY

—

FONTANA / RANCHO CUCAMONGA

Her dad gripped the wheel like it might try to jump out of his hands. He drove slow, used his signal when they moved from one lane to another or made a turn. He didn't say a word. He parked in the lot for one of those big sports stores where you could buy anything from a baseball to a canoe.

"Sit tight," he said. "Anybody messes with you, hold down the horn. I'll listen for it."

She watched him walk into the store. She realized she needed to pee, bad. She guessed she'd needed to for a while but had been too worried to notice. She chewed on her thumb, found a nub of flesh close to the nail, sunk her teeth in, tugged it loose with a red jolt of pain. She kicked her feet against the dashboard, *thud thud thud*. She dug into her backpack, found her new library books. She found one on UFOs. Polly liked reading about outer space, which made sense, seeing how she was from Venus.

She had been nine—three years after her dad went away, the

year he quit writing to her—when she'd decided she was born on
Venus. She didn't for real think she was from another planet—
Polly knew just where she came from, and she didn't believe in
aliens. But she was from Venus all the same.

She figured it out about the time she quit doing her homework. The first time she didn't do it, it was just because she forgot.
Ms. Phillips, her fifth-grade teacher, had kept her inside during
recess as punishment, which of course it wasn't. Polly, who was
mostly just playground prey to the other kids, sat happily at her
desk with her books as recess raged outside. She didn't read her
schoolbooks, which were so boring and stupid it made her want
to yank out chunks of her own hair. She read what she wanted to
read. She learned more during recess than she ever did in class.
She swore to herself never to do homework again.

One day the next week the principal came to Ms. Phillips's
classroom to take Polly away. She remembered their footsteps
impossibly loud in the hallway, that forbidden feeling of walking
through school when classes were going. He took her to a room
where a woman in a white sweater asked her to sit down across
the table from her. Polly remembered the way the woman had
lipstick on her teeth, how it made her look like a vampire who
had just fed.

The vampire had Polly solve mazes while timing her. She
showed Polly lists of words and asked what they had to do with
each other. She had Polly fit blocks together.

"She shows me this chart, right?" Mom had said later in the
car. "Like this," and she traced a hump in the air with a chipped
blue nail, "and she said it was a belt curve that shows how smart
people are. Most people are in the middle, she said. Seems to me
most people are on the dumb side, but whatever. She said that

retarded people—she didn't say retarded but she meant retarded—
are all the way on the left of the curve. And she said you, you're all
the way on the right."

She side-eyed Polly when she said it, like this was a secret Polly
had kept from her. Polly felt herself twisting on the inside. She
kept her eyes on her book, on a picture of Venus. It was a pale
white pearl hanging in space. It looked so calm. *Tranquil* was the
word the book used, and that was a good word, wasn't it?

Polly kept reading, and the book said that while Venus looked
tranquil, that was just how it looked from the outside. When you
got to Venus what you learned was that that calm surface was really clouds of acid, and underneath that tranquil sky was nothing
but jagged rock and howling windstorms. Polly read about this
pearl planet with a storm inside it and the thought burped full-
formed out of Polly's brain: *I'm from Venus.* That was the way Polly
felt, that outside she was quiet and calm but inside her acid winds
roared. She'd never known why she'd been that way, so quiet on
the outside but inside so screaming loud, but now she knew.

I'm from Venus.

Maybe this was the thing, the reason her brain didn't seem to
work the way other people's brains worked. Why it never stopped
moving. The reason she couldn't talk to people free and easy the
way others did. The reason the other kids pushed her away. They
could smell she was from Venus, even though she wasn't really. It
didn't matter that it wasn't real. It only mattered that it was true.

Now, in the sports store parking lot, Polly's Venus-child brain
kept yelling the same questions over and over.

*Why had her dad come to get her? Why was he driving a stolen car?
Why did he look over his shoulder all the time? Where was Mom?*

Even if he hadn't broken out, even if this car wasn't stolen,

Polly knew Mom's feeling about her dad well enough to know that she would never send him to pick up Polly. She'd have sent their neighbor Ruth or she would have called the school, or even woken Polly's night-shift-working stepfather Tom up from his day sleep to come get her.

Run, her brain told her. *Get out the car and go. Mom wouldn't want you here.*

Polly put the books and the bear into her backpack. She put her hand on the car door handle. A long moment passed. She couldn't move because of something inside her, something battened down under the acid winds. Her dad came out of the store, a plastic bag in his hands. Polly took her hand off the door handle. She'd let the ideas whip around inside her, but outside she'd done nothing. She was from Venus.

THEY DROVE SQUINTING against the setting sun. He checked them into a motel in Rancho Cucamonga, on the other side of the Speedway. He stopped on the way and bought them fast food.

The motel room smelled like burnt rubber. The sun was low-slung in the sky. It shone orange through the windows, turning her dad into a big black shape framed by light as he shut the door behind them. Polly went fast to the bathroom and peed, worried he could hear the splashes.

She came back to find her dad emptying the sports store bag onto the table by the door. Polly fished chicken nuggets out of the fast-food bag and sat on the bed. She put the straw of her orange drink to the bear's snout. The bear rubbed its belly with a paw like *yum.*

One by one her dad laid out the things he had bought. A kid-sized metal baseball bat. A black hoodie and black sweatpants. A black ski mask. A long, wicked-looking hunting knife that seemed to hiss like a snake at Polly.

He picked up the kiddie bat, flipped it so he held the fat end. He held the skinny end toward Polly.

"Come on and take it," he said. She swallowed a lump of chicken nugget, suddenly huge in her throat as she tried to get it down. She took the bat. It was cold in her hands. It made her realize she was burning up. He pulled the cushion off the chair in the corner and held it up.

"Want you to take a swing at this," he said. She looked back to the bear like he could save her, but of course he couldn't.

"Forget the bear," her dad said, his eyes like *you better not mess around*. "Show me what you got."

She swung. It felt jerky and wrong. The bat glanced off the cushion with a dull puff. Gym-class nightmares played in her head. Memories of kids watching her with bored cruel eyes while she struggled to do a sit-up, failed to turn a cartwheel.

"Aw, come on," her dad said. "That's not gonna do."

He got down on his knees next to her so that she could smell the salt and stink of him. Her brain threw out a handful of half-formed memories that were all knotted up in that smell. He took her elbows in his rough hands. He grabbed an ankle and pulled it to widen her stance. She lost balance, caught herself on his shoulder, moved her hand away fast.

"Come on now," he said. "You got to spread your base there. You got to swing your body, not your arms."

She swung again. The same clumsy feeling. The same puff. He shifted. He made a noise. Gym-class flashbacks intensified. She swung again. Another whiff. He tossed the pillow aside. She saw that he was angry and trying to hide it. Inside her, acid hurricanes swirled.

"That's enough," he said. "When I leave, you block that door. Shove a chair underneath the knob or something. Don't let anyone but me in."

He knocked twice, paused, knocked three times.

"That's the sign. If I don't knock like that, don't even let me in. If someone kicks their way in, you swing that bat at them, right in their knee. Swing hard. Swing through that son of a bitch. That should make 'em bend over a little bit. Then you swing that bat at their head hard as you can."

He might as well have told her to fly.

"I can't—"

"I said hard as you can. Don't hide under the bed or any of that stupid shit. People know to look under beds. Just hit them and run your ass off. You see anyone—I'm talking anyone—has a blue tattoo of a thunderbolt on their arm, you hit them and you hit them again. You don't stop swinging till they stop moving."

She'd never been so aware of how much of her body was blood. She was overstuffed with it. She felt her pulse everywhere, throbs in the tips of her fingers, her heart like a boot in her chest, rushes and roars in her ears. She had so much blood there wasn't any room for air.

"Blue lightning. On their arm," he said. "That means they're bad dudes, so cracking their heads ain't a sin. Now do what I said."

He picked up the bag and went into the bathroom. Outside the night had come. The door to it sat four steps from Polly. She did not move toward it. He came out wearing the black sweats and hoodie. The ski mask was in one pocket. The knife was in the other.

"And you stay in this room," he said. "I'm for real. This is life and death, you hear me?"

Fear like drowning came over Polly.

"Don't go," she said. Letting the words out almost let out all the things storming in her. The things she swallowed back made a hard lump in her throat.

"Shit," he said, "I know you're scared. I'm not gonna lie to you and tell you not to be scared. There's things going on, hard things. I got my reasons for doing this the way I'm doing. But I'm gonna make it okay. I'm gonna—"

And then he stood there like maybe he was going to say something else, or maybe come to her, hold her and hug her like he hadn't in years, but he didn't. He just stood there looking at the floor.

"Please." She wanted to scream it but it came out a rasp.

"Don't stop swinging," he said, and then he left.

Polly stood in the dark. Every sound in the night bounced off her like she had bat sonar. She walked to the door and put her hand on the knob. She closed her eyes. In her head she saw faceless men wearing blue lightning tattoos and teeth like yellow saw blades.

I can't run. I can't.

She turned away from the door. She picked up the baseball bat and placed it in the bed next to her. She rolled on her side. She held the bear in her arms. The bear petted her arm with one grubby paw like *there there, there there*. It made her feel better. It didn't matter the bear wasn't real. It only mattered that he was true.

3

NATE
—
FONTANA

Finding his ex-wife Avis this way, knife-dead in the dark on the bedroom floor next to her new man, didn't tell Nate everything he needed to know. It was the scrim of cigarette ash on top of the beer can on the living room table that gave Nate the answer he'd been looking for. The answer to the question that echoed in his head over and over, a question that came from the ghost of his brother Nick.

Are they hunting her?

He hadn't known when he'd left Polly at the motel and gone and broke into his Avis's house that the ashy beer can was what he'd come to see. He thought he'd come to see Avis's dead body, and he had, but that had only given him part of the answer he needed. It told him he was damned, that staying alive this long he'd doomed Avis and her new man. But it didn't tell him what to do next.

NATE HAD NEVER known his father—he'd fallen to death in a construction site accident when Nate was four—so his brother Nick had been the one to teach him. Not school stuff, which of course was bullshit, but instead stuff about the world, and being a man in that world. Nick taught Nate how to talk and how to fight, when lies were okay and when lies were not. He'd taught him the strongest thing you could do was take more than your share of pain. He'd dragged him to a gym when he was eleven and taught him how to take a punch, how to swallow the sting of it. He'd taken him when he was sixteen to a liquor store and given him a pistol and a mask and taught him how to rob, and how it felt good to do it, and that a job was a dishonorable thing, and that the better thing was to take what you needed when you needed it. He'd steered Nate so much that by the time Nate went to jail and was separated from his brother, he had Nick in his head to tell him what to do, and even later when Nick died, his voice in Nate's head was strong as ever, strong enough that Nate didn't know who he'd be without it there.

ARE THEY HUNTING HER?

Avis's husband had had his skull crushed, facedown on the bed in his underwear, like they'd caught him sleeping. The bedroom where Nate found them had taped-shut windows and a white noise machine, signs of a day sleeper. Nate remembered he worked third shift at the battery factory.

They must have done him first. Avis had died fighting here on the floor, kitchen knife in hand. The way her body had been twisted, the way her face looked away from him so he could see the star tattoo on her neck, those were things Nate knew would never leave him now.

THEY'D BEEN DRUNK, summer daytime drunk, the best kind of drunk there was, the day she got that star tattoo. They were in an electric, bruising kind of young love, the best kind of love there was. She was a waitress in a chain restaurant. He sold weed and sometimes stuck up places with his brother Nick. She said she liked that he was an outlaw, but sometimes her eyes said something different.

They'd taken his old Dodge convertible to the quick shop— Nate and Nick had robbed this very one a month earlier, and knowing that added to the thrill for the both of them—for big plastic cups of ice and Coke and a pint bottle of whiskey. They drank half the Coke too fast, getting ice cream headaches, before topping the rest off with whiskey. On the way to the tattoo parlor he'd asked her why she wanted a star, and why on her neck? She'd smiled and said it was special to her, and she'd tell him someday, and he hadn't pushed her about it because they had time to spare because they weren't ever going to die.

He held her hand while the tattoo guy needled the star just below where the spine plugged into the skull. He let her lie about it not hurting. Afterward, sweaty from the sun as they drove with the top down back toward Fontana, she fingered the fresh clean gauze on her neck and smiled her rocket smile and said they needed to pull over. He drove them up into the hills. They went at each other before the car came to a full stop. As Nate rocked into her, he lifted his head up in the air like triumph. He looked up and saw a condor circling overhead, watching to see if they were dead. He remembered how he'd felt her skin rubbing slick against his own and saw the animal in her eyes and thought they'd never die. Not today, not ever.

NOT TODAY, NOT EVER, he thought, standing over her corpse. His fingers grasped useless air. He wanted to choke the world if he only could find its fucking neck.

The anger in him, though. It's what did this in the first place. His anger at anyone who ever tried to force his hand or tell him what to do.

I should have let Chuck gut me. I could have died for my own sins back in Susanville.

I ought to go upstairs and find her new man's guns and find out what a gun barrel tastes like.

But he couldn't. Nate had fucked up everything in his life, starting the day he let his brother Nick take him on a stickup job, and following with almost every choice he'd made since then. He'd fucked himself from jump street. He knew that and he owned it, and he knew with Avis and her man dead because of what he'd done, he was unredeemable, and the king-hell irony of it was his death was a fair price to pay, and he'd pay it if he could, but he couldn't just yet. Not until he knew the answer.

Are they hunting her?

And the other, darker questions.

Do you have to stay alive? Or do you have to die?

One question followed the other. The greenlight that Crazy Craig had issued naming Nate a dead man had named Avis and Polly too. He'd read it in Susanville on the eve of his release, his eyes going back to the same lines, the lines that said *he has a woman*

he has a daughter

But would they really kill a girl? Even if Avis was dead, and Nate too, would these berserkers actually come gunning for a child? That's what Nate had to know before he knew what to do next.

He knew the ashy beer can was the sign when he saw it. He knew it because he knew Avis. He knew her old man had been the kind of smoker they don't even make anymore, the kind with yellow fingers and an ashtray in the shower. And Nate knew how Avis figured that's where her asthma came from, and that she hated cigarettes and smoke. She'd never tolerate a smoker in the house. So when Nate found the beer can on the coffee table next to the easy chair, that's when he knew. Whoever'd ashed in the beer can had done it after Avis was dead. And Nate knew Aryan Steel cowboys were cold-blooded, but not even one of them would have stuck around for a smoke after a double murder. Not unless they had a reason. Not unless they were waiting for something. Or someone.

he has a daughter

The beer can meant Aryan Steel were going to be true to their word. They were hunting for Polly. That was Nate's fault, and if he could pay for it with his life he would have. But that wasn't on the table. First he had to get Polly up to Stockton with his cousins. Then he'd turn his anger out on the world, onto Aryan Steel, and get them to lift the greenlight on her. He stood there in the dark, feeling something that was sort of like relief. The days ahead were bad, but at least now he knew what the answers were.

Are they hunting her?

Yes.

Do you have to stay alive?

Until I save this girl I've damned.

He left Avis and her new man where they lay. He owed her better than that, but he didn't have a choice. He went upstairs to pack a bag for Polly and see if Avis's new man had any guns.

4

POLLY

—

ANTELOPE VALLEY

He'd been to her house. He didn't think she knew. But she recognized the scuff on the suitcase he'd carried out to the car that morning. The scuff had happened last summer, when her stepdad Tom had dropped it down a flight of stairs in Big Bear when they'd gone up there to look at the snow. It was her stepdad's suitcase. That meant that her dad had been to her house, and either her mom knew she was with her dad, or . . . or something else, something her brain kept from her for now. Something big as Venus and heading her way.

They'd driven out of the Empire, gone up a hill so steep Polly's ears popped, and then went down the other side, where there wasn't much but alfalfa farms and fields. The land to the left of the road was covered in a thick carpet of yellow poppies. Poppies were dreaming flowers, like the kind that put Dorothy to sleep in that weird part of *Wizard of Oz*. Polly knew better than to wish this was a dream.

"We're gonna see a woman named Carla. Big Carla? You remember her?"

She shook her head like *no*.

"She's an old friend of me and your mom's. Back when we had friends in common. She works at a gas station up here. Big Carla's gonna get you up to Stockton so I can take care of some business. My cousin Zach, he's gonna take you in. You stay there and you'll be safe. Safe as anywhere, anyway."

"I want to go back to Mom."

Her dad kept his hands on the wheel and his eyes on the road. She looked at a vein on the side of his forehead. Polly didn't know if it had always been there but she didn't think so.

"We get you up to Stockton, with our cousins," he said. "That's the thing."

She wondered what would happen if she jumped from the car. Would she skip down the side of the road like a flat stone on a lake or skid to a stop right where she landed? She looked down at a red row of nail marks on her arms. She'd tilled her arm without even noticing it. It was like the stuff that swirled inside her that she kept under so well was starting to scratch the surface. Polly knew that couldn't happen. She couldn't let it out, ever, or something bad would happen. That's why she had to keep the storm inside her. She had to keep it in. She ground her teeth together. The bear kissed his paw and pressed it to the scratches. She hugged him so tight.

The gas station sat across the road from an alfalfa farm. The store had a sign above it, SUNSHINE MARKET, with a sunglass-wearing sun waving above the name. He pulled them into the gravel lot. He steered the car into the patch of shade laid down by a wooden tank of water held up by wooden slats.

White gravel threw up light and heat, poking Polly's eyes on the walk to the front of the store. She stumbled against her dad, snapping back away before he could reach out to help her.

It was two seasons colder inside the store. A man with a creased cowboy hat and a cannonball gut scratched lotto tickets at the counter with a thick brown thumbnail. Two rows of junk food divided the store. In the back where the cold drinks were a young man in a trucker cap loitered looking at canned beer. He snuck a peek at Polly that made gooseflesh pop on her arms, or maybe it was just the cold air. She peeked at the man again but he'd gone back to looking at the beer.

The woman behind the counter might have been her dad's age or ten years older. Her dad had called her Big Carla. It fit. She was big all over, from her boobs spilling out of her motorcycle T-shirt and her round arms to her round brown eyes and teased-up hair.

"Good to see you, honey," she said to her dad. She reached over the counter for an awkward hug. Polly watched her dad take it stiffly. He didn't like being touched any more than Polly did, she could tell.

Big Carla's voice went up an octave as she turned back to Polly. "Hey there," she said. "My name's Carla. I haven't seen you since you were a baby. Look at how you grew."

Polly never knew what to say to stuff like that. Her eyes switched focus to the wall behind Carla. It was covered with checks, CANCELED stamped in red ink. DEADBEATS scrawled on a note card above them. She knew what a deadbeat was, but seeing it there scrawled in red ink it looked to Polly like a word for a horrible thing, a nightmare thing. All at once Polly was very sure that there was something terrible here. Terrible and unstoppable.

"You're gonna spend the day with me," Carla said. Her smile spread across her face like a billboard. "And after I'm done with work we're gonna take a car trip. Does that sound like fun?"

Polly wanted to say *no*. But of course she didn't.

"Oh, you're shy, huh, hon?"

That was another one adults asked that Polly never knew what to say to.

"Go get a soda or something," her dad said to her. "Let me talk to Carla here."

Polly walked down the chip aisle toward the coolers in the back. She ran her fingers across the plastic bags of corn chips and pork rinds just to hear the rustle of them. The grown-ups pitched their voices low and urgent. Like what Mom and Tom would do when they didn't want Polly to know they were arguing. She stopped halfway down the aisle, tried to listen to them talk over the haw of the air conditioner.

"This ought to cover her for a while," her dad said. "I'll come for her when she's safe."

"This dirty?"

"What money ain't? Shit, take it. I can get more."

"Where's Avis, Nate?"

Polly could smell something coppery. Maybe the hot dogs spinning on their rack, but she didn't think that's what it was.

"Never you mind."

"Nate—"

"You don't want to be any deeper in this thing than you are right now," he said. "Don't ask me questions you don't want the answer to."

"All right," Carla said.

"I got things to do and I can't have a girl with me when I do them," he said. "Now you said you'd take her to Stockton—"

"I'll take her," Carla said. "Damn you, Nate, I'll take her. But just settle down a minute. Let me get you some food or something."

Polly tried to get her machine-gun pulse under control. Tried to remember how to breathe. The something inside her that she was trying not to feel, it was growing, growing bigger even than her, and she looked over to the hot dogs with their skin split from overcooking and she felt like she was going to split open like that.

Don't ask me questions you don't want the answer to.

The man in the trucker hat reached out to close the cooler door. The sleeve of his T-shirt rode up. It showed off a tattoo on his shoulder, a blue zigzag like cartoon lightning.

Blue lightning.

The man walked past her and out the door, no beer or anything in his hands. He got into his car and started it, but didn't leave. He got on his phone instead.

She went to her dad and reached out to touch him. Her hand stopped just short of his arm but he saw her anyway.

"Girl, thought I told you to leave us be."

She touched her bicep and said, "Blue lightning. On his arm. You said—"

It happened so fast. Polly followed her dad's eyes to Carla. Carla's smile slid off her face. Carla bolted. Her dad grabbed Carla by the hair. The cowboy with the scratcher tickets said, "What the fuck?" He ran out the door. His scratchers floated to the floor behind him. Time must have been doing weird stuff, because Polly could follow every flutter and flip of the tickets as they headed for the floor. Her dad said, "Goddamn it." He pulled the pistol out of his pocket. He said, "Who'd you tell?" He put the gun to Carla's head.

"Oh god, don't kill me," Carla said.

Polly's body ran without her telling it. The slap of her feet on the floor rocketed up her legs as she moved as fast as she could for the outside.

"Polly—" he yelled after her.

She hit the door bear first. Sun blindness squeezed her eyes closed. The man with the tattoo came out of nowhere.

"Hey there, sugar."

Polly saw a glitter in his hand. Her brain screamed *knife*. Her muscles locked up on each other. The wind hissed in her ears. The light from the blade flashed. It danced, like how a cobra danced.

A strong arm scooped her up from behind. Her father's smell filled her nose. He held her in one arm. He pointed his pistol at the man with the other.

Polly felt wet warmth in her pants. Behind the man with the knife, cars rolled past same as always. On the other side of the road poppies swayed in the breeze like the world hadn't just shattered into a million pieces. Like somehow the world still made any kind of sense at all.

"Drop it," her dad said.

The man raised his hands, dropped the knife onto the gravel.

"Kick it," her dad said, and the man kicked the knife out of reach.

"Got a message for the Steel," her dad said. "You tell them to stop coming."

"Heard we got your woman already," the man said.

Polly felt her dad's legs give way a bit, felt him tighten the squeeze on her.

"That's one for one," her dad said. "You tell them we're even. Tell them to let it be."

"You think you can turn this around?" the man asked. "Hell, you're already dead. You're a goddamn zombie walking."

The man pointed at Polly.

"You and her both."

For a second they all just hung in space as the rumble of far-away thunder on a clear day filled the air. Her dad cocked his head toward the sound.

"You call in cavalry?" he asked.

The guy smiled like *damn right*.

"We won't be here when they get here," her dad said. "You tell 'em they'll lose more than they'll win."

"You're the one with the gun, hoss," the man said. "But you got the whole world after you. Can't kill the world."

Her dad never turned his back on the man as he walked them back to the car. Polly kept her eyes on the smiling man until her dad shoved her into the car and she had to scramble to the passenger seat before he crushed her.

THEY DROVE OUT heading back the way they came. The roar of clear-sky thunder grew louder. Four men on motorcycles came the other way, their skin dirty with ink and scars, black leather on their backs. Polly turned as they passed, saw their back patches, a bearded one-eyed man, the words ODIN'S BASTARDS.

Polly came back to herself enough to notice the damp patch at her crotch. She should have felt shame, she knew that, but that other thing, the thing she'd been stuffing down, was the only thing left in her anymore.

Her brain looped the man's voice. *Heard we got your woman already*. The voice mixed with everything else in her head. Her brain put it all together. It did not let her hide from what she already knew.

"Did you kill my mom?" somebody inside her asked out loud.

"No," her dad said.

"She's dead, though," somebody inside her said.

The look he gave her was the only answer she needed, but he said it anyway.

"Yeah. Polly, I'm sorry—"

The thing inside her came out in a war cry. She grabbed the door handle. She popped it open. She looked out at the speed-blurred gravel. She jumped.

5

NATE

—

ANTELOPE VALLEY

The volume of the world turned up as Polly got her door open. Before he could even put together what she was doing she jumped feetfirst.

Both Nate's hands left the wheel on pure instinct before his brain could think anything other than *holy shit*. He leaned across the car. His hand snagged hair. The hair went taut as her bottom half left the car. Her shoes skipped against the asphalt. He yanked. She came halfway back inside. Nate got his left hand on the wheel. Looked up at the road. They'd drifted across the center line. A flatbed loaded with migrant workers rushed at them. Nate yanked Polly inside the car. She yelped with pain. He spun the wheel. That weird floating feeling in his gut and his balls as the car twisted. They headed toward the side of the road.

The car coughed up gravel dust as they slid to a stop on the shoulder. Polly let loose another one of those animal sounds, something way past grief. The screams turned to tears. She wept

so her whole body shook with electric-shock tremors. They sat at
the side of the road as Polly wrung herself dry. Nate watched her
weep, knowing he should reach out to her, hold her. But he didn't
know how. It wasn't the sort of thing Nick had taught him. So he
just drove.

After she'd emptied herself she slept curled against the car
door out of his reach. She held her bear death-grip tight, smear-
ing tear-snot across the top of his head.

He watched the girl from the corner of his eyes, like his full
gaze might wake her. The only parts of himself he saw in her were
her eyes and the buried rage she'd just shown him.

He didn't know if the old cowboy had called the cops, or if the
pack of Odin's Bastards would come back down the road hunting him. All he knew was that he had only one thing left in his
life, and that was keeping this girl safe. He saw now that send-
ing her to Stockton couldn't happen. She was no safer there than
anywhere else. He couldn't drop her off with the law, and not just
because the ghost of his brother in his head would never allow
it. Group homes and orphanages were no safer than the streets.
They were cages full of predators and Polly was prey.

NATE KNEW HOW DANGEROUS cages could be. He'd done five years with
his head down. The sharks knew his brother. Nick the stickup
king. Nick the killer. The name bought Nate safe haven, even after
Nick died. His reputation was so good it left background radia-
tion. Later on, Nate figured that the safe passage had fucked him.
He'd never had to fight, so it looked like he couldn't. If he'd let the
anger out even once in those first five years, maybe Chuck Hollington never would have made his move.

Like a lot of the bad news in Nate's life, it started out looking like good news. An appeal his court-appointed lawyer had filed, an appeal Nate hadn't even paid mind to, had sprung fruit. Misdated statements, a prosecutor willing to take a time-served plea-down to preserve his conviction rate. Nate only cared about the bottom line: freedom suddenly loomed. He thought about getting a job. Maybe at a gym. He'd helped Nick train for his fights. Maybe that was something he could do.

Now, with Polly sleeping next to him, he wanted to lie to himself, to say he had planned that once he was free he was going to make things right and get to know this little girl. But he hadn't. He had barely thought of her at all until he read the death warrants.

A week before Nate was set to walk free, Ground Chuck Hollington found him taking a mop break behind the boilers. Chuck had a smile that would make a kid scream. A soda-bottle meth cooker had blown up in his face a few years back, leaving his left cheek pink raw hamburger. That's when "Ground" got added to the Chuck. Chuck had two blue thunderbolt tats on his left bicep. Aryan Steel soldiers got a blue bolt for each kill they made for the gang. Chuck was brother to Crazy Craig Hollington, president of Aryan Steel, the man who ruled the whiteboy world from his isolation cell in Pelican Bay. He hadn't said boo to Nate in the past five years. Now he stood next to him behind the boiler, an inked hand raised for a fist bump. Nate gave it to him.

"What's good?" Nate asked.

"Heard you're short-timing."

"A week." The conversation was like a walk across a rotten wooden bridge. Nate could feel the wood wanting to break, each word a step.

"You hooked up? Someone on the street gonna set you right?"

"I got some shit cooking," Nate lied.

"You know about the garage?" Chuck asked him.

Nate knew about the garage. Susanville had an auto shop. Convicts worked it. Prison employees got a discount. They patronized it exclusively. Chuck had noticed. He'd had a brainstorm. When a hack made an appointment for an oil change, the Aryan Steel hanger-on who worked the garage desk sent word down the line. The night before the appointment, an outside man went to the hack's house, found his car, taped a bag of dope or whatever to the inside of the hack's wheel well. The hack drove his car into the shop. A convict-mechanic would take off the bag while changing the oil. The scam turned the hacks into mules.

"Dude we had on the outside just got pinched," Chuck said. "Pigs came into his house on a domestic, guess he'd tuned up his girl something proper, and the dumb motherfucker had left his pipe on the table. Pigs tossed the place and found a whole grip of shit."

Chuck let Nate do the math. They needed a new man on the outside. Nate was heading outside. Pretty simple math.

Taking the job meant jumping from one prison right into another, one with invisible walls. Aryan Steel never paroled you, never let you loose with time served. It was a life sentence. Nate weighed his options, heard the creak of rotten wood in his head. He knew what the ghost of his brother would have him do. He put his weight down.

"Know what, I'm good," Nate said. "Think I'm going to see what the world has to offer me."

Chuck changed posture, stepped his left foot forward, turned his body so his side faced Nate. Unconscious things a fighting man does when he thinks blood is coming. Nate mirrored him. Fight-flight jet fuel made muscles twitch at random. He took three deep breaths, the way Nick taught him. The air felt hot down his throat, but it settled him.

"Dude, I don't know what made you think I was asking," Chuck said. "I'm telling you what's going to go down."

That's when he heard the words. Heard them like Nick wasn't dead, like he was right there in Nate's skull. Nate let them come out his mouth knowing how stupid it was.

"Fuck you, bitch." He popped a middle finger in Chuck's face.

The shank came out of nowhere. Nate grabbed the knife-wrist. His other hand grabbed Chuck's billy-goat beard. He put his foot behind Chuck's. He twisted his hips. He slammed Chuck onto the floor. Chuck's skull *thocked* against the concrete. He followed Chuck down. He drove his knee into Chuck's liver. He bent Chuck's arm at the elbow. He pressed the shank point at the hollow of Chuck's throat. Flesh dimpled at the shank's point. One drop of blood bloomed.

Nate knew the smart thing was to let Chuck go. Leave him alive, dodge Aryan Steel for a week, and walk out a free man. He thought that was the smart play, kept thinking it even as he pushed the blade down into Chuck.

The shank went through the neck. Shock waves bounced back into Nate's arm as the shank point bounced off concrete. Chuck died with scared eyes and a mouth full of blood foam. The last thing he saw was Nate's middle finger.

Nate took three deep breaths. He took in what he'd done. He had never killed before. Like a lot of things in life, it didn't feel as big as you thought it would. He washed his hands in his mop bucket. He headed back into the hallway. Nobody around. He finished his mopping and was back in his cell by the time they found the body and locked the prison down.

That night he studied the roof of his cell. He couldn't tell if the bridge had collapsed under him or if he'd made it to the other side. He didn't know if he was floating or falling. He figured he wouldn't know until he hit the bottom.

Investigations happened, plural. DOC Special Services detectives with bad sports coats and paunches came through first. They locked the place down for a full week. They questioned everyone. Cons snitched to their own advantage. They snitched drug-turf rivals. They snitched cons they owed big money to. They snitched on the guy in the next cell with the screaming meemie night terrors just to get a good night's sleep. The hacks made zero progress. They weren't the ones ruining Nate's sleep anyway.

Aryan Steel did their own investigation. Word came down from Pelican Bay. News had reached the isolation cells of Supermax. Crazy Craig had learned his brother had been killed. He ordered the knifeman found. A peckerwood killer named Dog—four blue bolts on his arm, an Othala rune above his heart, a long and jagged thumbnail on his left hand—took Chuck's crown in Susanville with Crazy Craig's blessing. Nate heard about Dog's investigation one night around the card table. Dog knew a Black Guerilla Family soldier named Cocaine who had squabbled with Chuck. Dog used his long thumbnail to gouge out Cocaine's eye. Cocaine confessed to the kill—of course he did. Dog got Cocaine to tell it again. Cocaine got his facts wrong. Dog knew a phony confession when he heard one. It's the ones who get the details right, even when you hurt them close to death, that are the guilty ones. They left Cocaine bleeding and half blind, bringing another lockdown prison-wide.

Nate counted days, wondered if he'd gotten away clean. When he got to the day before his release, he figured he'd made it out clear. Then it all came crashing down. A kid named Lewis, a nineteen-year-old nobody—the kind of scared whiteboy who swam by the side of Aryan Steel like pilot fish by a shark—gave Nate the warning that saved his life. Nate was never sure why. Maybe it was how Nate always gave the kid his dessert when Nate was eating clean. Something small like that. He came to Nate in his cell. He pressed a piece of paper into Nate's hand.

"Don't come out till you read it," he whispered.

It was a photocopied kite. Nate read it, each word ratcheting up his heartbeat.

> to all solid soldiers on the block
> or in the streets
> open season on the race traitor
> who got my brother
> I here his name is Nate McClusky
> he is getting sprung soon
> full greenlight on the knifeman
> he has a daughter named Polly
> he has a woman named Avis
> I here they are in Fontana
> full greenlight on his woman
> full greenlight on their seed
> they should die by blade
> salt the earth
> all who refuse to help are added to the greenlight
> membership guaranteed for those who complete it
> franchise guaranteed for those who complete it
> crazy craig, president
> steel forever, forever steel

He didn't know how they knew. He didn't know why Lewis had warned him. But those were questions that didn't matter, and Nate only had time now for things that mattered very much.

he has a daughter

Nate stayed in his cell, his back to the wall. He spent that night waiting for the kill to come. Every step on the walkway outside his cell shook through him like electric shocks.

Around midnight a voice bounced in from someplace in the cellblock.

"Jump off the tier and save us some time, motherfucker."

"I always wanted to see if a whiteboy could fly," some Mexi con yelled.

"You dead already, Nate," a hoarse voice—Nate pegged it as Dog—yelled. "You just a zombie walking is all."

Laughs. Cheers. The chant caught on. *Zombie walking, zombie walking.*

Morning came. The hacks handcuffed Nate for his last walk off the tier. A last-second assassination not out of the question. But it didn't come. Best Nate could figure, they just hadn't had time to set it up proper.

Zombie walking. The words rang out in the voice of a hundred hardened cons.

Zombie walking.

He got processed. They gave him his old clothes and three hundred dollars gate money. He tasted free air. He found a pay phone to call Avis. The number came up dead. Of course she'd changed it in the last five years. He found a car old enough that he knew how to hotwire it. He busted the window to get in. He got it started with a screwdriver. From release to felony in eighteen minutes. That had to be a record.

NOW, ON THE ROAD out of Antelope Valley, Nate pulled to the side of the road just off the highway off-ramp, where the 138 met the 14, as Polly slept grief-exhausted next to him. He weighed options. He was back on that wooden bridge. This time it was worse. This time he had a little girl strapped to his back.

She was strapped to him, there was no escaping that. He saw that now. If nowhere was safe for her, then the only place he could let her be was with him. If they were going to fall, they'd fall together, and he didn't know what else he could give her than that.

6

POLLY

—

MOUNT VERNON / FONTANA

Polly lived her next days underwater. Noises sounded muffled, like she was hearing them through plugged ears. Her arms and legs moved slow and heavy. Lights turned to prisms in her eyes. She wasn't hot and she wasn't cold.

She didn't mind being underwater. She felt all sealed up, like one of those fish who could live at the bottom of the sea and carry the weight of the whole ocean on their backs without being crushed.

She thought about Mom. The way she snorted when she laughed, the way she flicked bottle caps across the room with snapping fingers. How she was dead now. It was because her dad's world had crashed back into hers that Mom was dead. She didn't know if she hated him or not. She was too far underwater to know.

They got a room in a different motel just like the last one. They stayed below the highway in Mount Vernon, where the Mexicans lived. Other white people made her dad nervous, made him touch the pistol he kept in his back pocket. She guessed Mexicans didn't wear blue thunderbolt tattoos.

They didn't talk unless they had to, which was fine with Polly. They watched teevee in the motel room. Her dad started the morning with push-ups and shadowboxing. Polly watched, but the bear lay face-first on the bed and did push-ups in time with her dad. They ate from trucks and taco stands. Polly couldn't eat more than a bite or two at a time. Her stomach felt small. Three bites max. The beans and tortillas tasted bland to her waterlogged tongue.

Her dad said they were waiting. He didn't say what they were waiting for. People had to know that she was gone. They had to be looking for her, didn't they? Maybe Maria from school, or even Mrs. Ray, her teacher. Or even the police. She was missing, she guessed. It seemed weird to think about. She wasn't missing. She was right where she was. She thought it was the police who were really missing. They were the ones who weren't where they were supposed to be, which was coming to get her. At night when her dad snored she thought about finding them herself, her and the bear slipping out the door. She might even have done it if she hadn't been underwater.

Their third night in the new motel, her dad said he was done waiting. He dressed in his dark clothes, the black hoodie. It made him look like a criminal, which Polly guessed made sense. He took out the pistol, which she now knew used to belong to her stepfather Tom. He popped it open so she could see the bullets' butts, he spun the barrel around, and then he slammed it shut. It wasn't how Tom treated his guns at all, the way he'd taught Polly to treat them, like they were living and treacherous things.

Somewhere else in the motel, a couple argued in Spanish.

The argument turned into screaming. There were crashes and crunches along with the screams. Someone yelled for *la policía*. Polly wondered if they should go help, but the thought seemed far away.

The fighting made her dad even more nervous. It made him touch his pocket where the gun was. He muttered curse words under his breath. He walked back and forth across the room. He threw punches in the air. He looked out the window. He turned back to Polly.

"Come on," he said. "You're coming with me."

THEY DROVE TO A BLOCK up against the edge of the mountains. Nate shut off the headlights. They rolled slow and silent like a submarine.

They stopped in front of the one house on the block with lights still burning. Pickup trucks and dirt bikes were parked out front. He shut off the engine and opened his door. Guitar fuzz drifted through the night, that kind of rock music that sounded like the bellows of sea monsters. Somewhere men were laughing, loud and loose. The kind of laughs that would have made Polly scared if she could feel anything at all.

"Stay here," Nate said. "No matter what you hear."

He stepped out of the car, pushed the door shut slow so it barely clicked at all. He walked toward the side of the house, hand in the hoodie pocket. On the gun, Polly thought. He moved around the side of the house and out of view.

She wanted to know where he was going with the gun. Before, she would have just thought it and then the fear would take over and she would just let the thought stay inside her. If a thought stays inside you, Polly wondered, did it matter that you thought it at all? But this time, because she was underwater, she didn't feel the fear she usually felt.

"Let's go," she said to the bear. The bear nodded at her and placed a paw to its muzzle like *shh*.

She opened her door and slipped out into the night. She looked down the street, lit in dots by stuttering streetlights that wound down the road and out of sight. She heard her dad's voice behind the house. She followed it, the air so summer thick she felt she could lift her feet off the ground and swim through it. Dead grass crunched under her feet.

Light spilled out one window on the side of the house. A shape moved inside. Polly moved toward it. It was a woman mixing cranberry juice and vodka. There was nothing but window screen between them. The woman picked up her drink and took a sip. She did the that's-strong-shimmy, just the way Polly's mom did it. The woman tipped in a little more cranberry cocktail and twirled the drink in her hand to stir it. The motions were all familiar to Polly, but not quite right, like echoes off a cliff wall. It seemed to Polly that it ought to have made her feel something, but it didn't.

Polly heard voices in the backyard. She moved away from the window. Her foot caught on uncoiled hose. She went down in sharp brown grass. She stayed down. She belly-crawled to the corner of the house to peek in the backyard, the bear tucked tight against her armpit.

Her dad stood with his back to her. He was a shadow in front of a big green grill in the center of the yard. Two men sat in lawn chairs close by. A chicken sat upright on the grill, beer bubbling from a can stuffed inside it.

One of the men was huge, with a white T-shirt that stretched over his rolls of fat. His earlobes had been stretched out so they hung off his ears like flabbergasted mouths. He had a swastika tattoo on his neck. Polly hadn't ever seen one outside a book before.

The other had a beard like a goat. He had eyes like a goat too. At least there was something in them that didn't seem like people eyes. He had a cup in his lap and brown dribble on his chin. He was shirtless against the heat. He had a coffin tattooed over his heart. He had a bottle of beer resting tucked between his legs.

"Nate," that one said. "Didn't know you were out."

"I'm out. How you been, Jake?"

"Surviving," the one called Jake said. He said it with a smile that wasn't a smile. Like smiling was just a trick he'd learned.

The fat one laughed like a dog, *arf arf arf.*

"Surviving," the fat one said. "Can't say that for everyone, can we?"

Polly felt something bubble inside her, rivers flowing under ice. She stood up. She walked out from the shadow of the house without even knowing what she was doing. She stood near the door that led to the back of the house. They didn't see her. She was out of the light and small besides. Standing there invisible made something flash through her, some kind of electric shock. It was the most she'd felt in days. It got stronger when her dad took the pistol out from his pocket. Polly watched the gun come out of her dad's pocket and point itself at the man, and Polly knew she should have been scared but she wasn't.

The chrome of the pistol glowed orange from the grill light. The fat man sat up in his lawn chair looking at the pistol. The one her dad called Jake didn't move, he just smiled that not-smile. Even in the dim Polly could see his teeth were lacquered brown with chaw resin. He lifted his cup to his lips and spat. Polly saw the tattoos on his arm. The two blue lightning bolts.

"There's a greenlight on me," her dad said.

"No shit."

"My daughter too."

"Yup."

"You okay with them killing a little girl?"

"Hey, man. I don't make the rules."

"You and my brother were always cool."

"That what you think? Shit, man, you really that dumb? Ain't nobody was cool with your brother. He was a scary motherfucker is all. You come here thinking me and him was friends, you're wasting your time."

The door next to Polly swung open and light spilled out into the yard. The men turned to face it. It felt like they were looking right at Polly. Something told her not to move. She'd read it in a book, predators see motion.

"Jake? Everything all right?" the woman with the cranberry drink called from the doorway.

"Tell her to go inside," her dad said.

"Get back in the house," Jake said.

"Who's that out there with you?"

"I said back in the house."

"Is that a gun? I'm calling the cops."

"The fuck you are. Get back in the house and stay there, you stupid bitch."

Polly watched the woman go inside, a fast walk, the kind of walk you did when you didn't want the other person to see your face change.

"You know who did Avis?" her dad asked Jake. Her mom's name made Polly take a step toward the men.

Jake raised his eyebrows like *maybe*.

The chicken dribbled beer into the grill. The fire flared. The dribbling beer hissed.

"Tell me who killed her."

"You did," Jake said. "You did when you stuck that knife into Crazy Craig's brother. That greenlight ain't ever going away. Do yourself a favor, kill yourself and the girl too. That way at least you can make it soft and easy. Cause when the Steel does it, it's going to go the other way."

Later on Polly couldn't believe just how fast her dad moved in that moment. The one named Jake sprung up fast like he'd been waiting for it to happen, but he was still too slow. Her dad hit him with the pistol. Polly saw red splashes in the dark. She bit down, snapped a skin chunk off the inside of her lip. She felt warm liquid in her mouth. She felt pain. But it was her pain, and she was glad for it.

Her dad got his two hands in Jake's hair and kneed him in the face. It made a hollow sound, almost funny. Polly felt the jolt of it inside her.

Jake slumped back into his chair. His face looked like an earthquake to Polly. He coughed red tobacco chaw mud. It slid down the front of his chest. It left a streak across the coffin. His eyes slam-danced in their sockets.

Polly kept waiting for the fear to come, the fear that made her run in Antelope Valley. But instead she inched closer, close enough to smell the stink of the fighting men. She was close enough that if the men hadn't been so locked in on each other they would see her, dark or no.

The fat one stood. Her dad turned the gun on him. The man sat back down too fast. He slapstick somersaulted as the chair flipped over. He stayed facedown on the grass.

"You know who done it," her dad said. "I need his name. I need to know where to find him. You're going to tell me."

"Fuck all that," Jake said. Polly guessed that's what it was anyway. It was hard to tell with the way the words came out of his torn mouth.

"You're going to tell me who did Avis."

Jake spat pink. Her dad kicked the grill. The chicken tumbled to the ground. It belched beer foam. The grill laid a glowing tongue of hot coals across the lawn.

The fat man said, "Oh shit."

Hot wind rustled Polly's hair. It made the dead grass scratch and tickle her ankles.

Her dad lifted Jake to his feet by the hair. He dragged him to the coals that sat smoking in the grass. He kicked Jake's foot out from under him, twisted his body, took him down again. Jake landed in the coals back-first. He *sizzled*.

Her dad held Jake onto the coals. The fat man said, "Fuck." Jake screamed. Nate let him up. Jake scrambled off the coals. A chunk of charcoal had cooked itself tight to Jake's back. Nate kicked it off. He picked up the cooler. He dumped ice and melt-water and a couple of floating empties onto Jake's back. The water *shushed* as it drenched cooking flesh.

"I need the name," her dad said.

Jake talked mushmouth. He spat red glop and curse words. He said something about magic. At least that's what Polly heard.

Magic done it.

Her dad let him go. The words meant something to him.

"Magic," her dad said like it wasn't crazy. He nodded like *that figures*. "Tell me where."

Jake said something Polly couldn't make out. Maybe an address?

"I find you're lying I'll be back," Nate said.

The sudden knowledge that they were done, that they'd see her soon, filled Polly. She went back around the side of the house and climbed back in the car. The wind had shifted. The night air blew cool now. She could hear bugs all around. She felt shivery, like how she felt coming out of cold water on a summer day. She ran her hands over her arms. The peach fuzz on her legs. Fingers through her hair to her scalp. She felt her face. That's when her fingers told her she was smiling.

7

POLLY

—

MOUNT VERNON

She and her dad slept through the sunlight the next morning. They woke up to loud knocks. He had the pistol in his hand so fast, he must have slept with it under his pillow.

He stood next to the door, gun in hand. He pulled back the blinds. They saw the old lady next to a maid's cart. Her dad made the pistol disappear.

He opened the door and blinked against the sunlight, waved her away. The woman spoke fast Spanish. Polly's dad looked at her dumb. He'd never picked it up, Polly guessed. Polly under-stood *un poco*.

"*No, gracias, senorita,*" she said. Her voice sounded funny to her. She'd barely spoken in days.

The maid nodded and left. Her dad tossed the pistol onto his bed and rubbed his face with his hands. Polly counted her teeth with her tongue. She thought about the man last night with his back in the coals, how it was a bad thing she knew and she knew she should have hated it but she didn't.

It had sprung a leak in something, watching what her dad had done that night, and the water had leaked out around her and she could feel things again. She missed her mom. It felt like if she could turn her head fast enough, she'd catch a glimpse of her in the corner of her eye. She tried to make sense of what had happened. How magic could have killed her mom. But nothing in her dad's face said *ask me*. He got on the floor, bursting grunts with each push-up. The bear rubbed sleep from its eyes, joined him.

They ate chorizo con huevos at a taco stand down the street. Food had its taste back. They didn't speak but to order. Around them the world hummed. Planes overhead left streaks in the dirty air. Polly thought about how the kindergarten kids used gray crayons to color in the sky.

She played with the bear. It put a paw over its eyes, moved its head like *I've got guard duty*. Vigilant against blue lightning tattoos.

A toddler at the next table waved at the bear. The bear waved back. It wiggled its butt at the kid. It waved a paw under its butt like *I farted*. It put the paw to its face and shook like *hahaha*. The little kid laughed. Polly laughed too. She looked over to her dad and he was smiling, his eyes on her. She tried to see what was inside his eyes when he looked at her. She held his look for as long as she could, which wasn't very long, but still. It was something.

That night in the motel room, he changed into his night outfit again and she knew it would happen again.

He shadowboxed. He hopped on the balls of his feet.

"I can't take you this time," he said to her. "Pack up. We're gonna move on when I get back."

She watched him go, feeling dumb panic, wanting to go,

wanting to know what she was missing, what could be worse than the night before. She felt antsy. She turned on the teevee to have something to look at. She killed the sound so she could listen for footsteps outside.

The teevee light flickered. It threw big moving shadows against the wall. The shadows gave Polly the heebie-jeebies. She channel-surfed. She found a nature show. Foxes stealing baby birds from a nest, crunching them, running away as the momma bird flew back too late. She hit the local news. She recognized the face floating next to the anchorman. It was her own face, blotchy with pixels.

Her thumb had already pressed the button, changing the channel to some car dealer ad. Polly switched back quick. It was her face all right, a school picture from two years back when she'd had those dumb bangs. The yellow words MISSING GIRL floated under her head.

The teevee flickered to a picture of her mom and Tom, a selfie from Angels Stadium bleacher seats last year on Tom's birthday. Her mom smiling the way she did with all her teeth and her eyes scrunched into extra smiles. Polly made a noise with her throat, all her air coming out of her at once.

The picture changed to a lady reporter with lots of makeup, microphone in hand, standing in front of Polly's house. There was yellow tape across her own front door like on cop shows. Seeing it on teevee made it feel more real than if she'd been standing there.

The picture flickered to a black-and-white photo of her dad, a sign with numbers hanging under his chin, his eyes black pits.

The news cut to an interview with an Asian man, thin, sharp cheekbones, bags under his eyes like he never slept. She guessed he was good looking. His lips moved. A name floated under him while he talked, DETECTIVE JOHN PARK.

A phone number popped up on the screen. TO HELP CALL floated over it. Polly said the number out loud. She said it again, and again, until it was stuck in her head.

The teevee turned to a truck commercial. Polly shut it off. She sat in the dark. She'd been numb for a while and now she wasn't. She didn't have a mom anymore and she didn't have a stepdad, and even though it snagged fishhooks in her throat when she thought it, she didn't really have a dad either. Not for true.

She hugged the bear to her chest. She knew he wasn't real. To tell the truth, she was glad he wasn't. It meant that he could never leave her. She hugged him so tight. Polly chanted the TO HELP number to herself. Her voice stretched and cracked. The bear reached up to her face, petted her cheek. His paw came back wet.

Polly put the bear down. She picked up the phone. She snorted back tear-watery snot. She said the TO HELP number while she dialed it.

8

PARK

—

ANTELOPE VALLEY

Park knew why wolves howled when they hunted. He'd learned it his first night as a cop over in San Bernardino. He and Stutz, his training officer, had come across a street race in the warehouse district. Lines of cars on either side of the road, dozens of faces mouthing *oh shit the cops*. Stutz pulled a hard U and came back around. The racers gunned off the line, away from them. The spectators jumped in their own cars and sped off into the night.

"Code three," Stutz told Park. Park flipped the switch. The night turned blue and red. Stutz mashed the gas. Park felt acceleration press him like sideways gravity. The siren howled out into the night and something else was howling too and it took a second for Park to realize it was him.

"Goddamn," he said, and Stutz had laughed and said, "You're goddamn right," and pretty soon they were laughing together, laughing at how crazy good it all was. They drove fast as falling. They ran their quarry to the ground. On a skidding turn when the tire squeals joined the choir, Park's skin went gooseflesh—hell, his soul went gooseflesh. The car they chased hit a bad turn, rolled and wrapped itself roof-first around the pole of a fast food sign. It made a sound like God clearing his throat, and Park felt something crest and break inside himself, something so strong he quick-checked the front of his trousers to make sure he hadn't shot in his pants.

The way he saw it, these were junkie times he was living in. Everybody hooked on something. Maybe dope or booze. Maybe pizza or half-gallon cups of soda or foods made up by guys in white coats. Maybe picking fights on the Internet or some game with electric jewels falling from the top of their phones. But everybody was a rat in a lab, everybody had something stuck in their skulls and a pedal to push that gave them a jolt. The best thing you could do in this world was find the thing that jolted you the most and killed you the least, and go after it hard. For him it was the chase. So he'd given himself up to it.

He'd learned to use the thrill as a divining rod. He went where it told him to go. He pressed where the thrill told him to press.

When the captain told him about the double murder, the buzz kicked in. When he learned the ex-husband was a fresh-sprung ex-con, the hairs on his arms stood at attention. And when the cop showed him the photo of the missing girl with the sad blue eyes, he knew he was hooked.

And right now, in this gas station out in Antelope Valley, the buzz was telling him this woman behind the counter with the horseshit eyes knew something.

PARK HAD SPENT DAYS since the captain threw the murder of Tom and Avis Huff to Major Crimes learning the ins and outs of Nate Mc-

Clusky. He spent zero time on non-Nate avenues. A con walks out of jail, and twelve hours later his ex-wife is dead and his daughter is missing? One plus one equaled two last time Park checked.

Tom had a pretty nice gun collection. Park got a list of the guns Tom had registered, compared it to the guns they found, and did a little more simple math. Whoever killed them—read *Nate McClusky*—had helped him or herself—read *him*—to a couple of pistols and a nice Ithaca pump shotgun.

Park read up on Nate. He didn't see anything that didn't tag Nate as a pure knucklehead. Two armed-robbery convictions, small-time gas station shit. He got lucky with the first one by being white and nineteen. The judge gave him a break. The second one was pretty heavy time. He had served five years and should have been locked up for another five at least, but there was some sort of fuckup. Park scanned the appeal that had let Nate walk. It was pure legalese horseshit.

Nate's mother and father were dead. One sibling, a brother named Nick, also dead. Nick McClusky. The name poked out at Park. He ran the brother. He got back a heavy file. Nick had a few pro MMA fights. Then he beat a man to death in a bar fight when he was twenty-three. It got pled as manslaughter. Nick did a bit in Victorville. Came out scarier. He did muscle work for Aryan Steel. He'd died a few years back, crashed a stolen bike on the freeway during a high-speed chase. The guy had died live on the evening news.

Park knew the odds were on Nate getting picked up on a traffic stop or doing another robbery. Odds were he'd get himself caught before Park would find him. Park chased the buzz and kept busy anyway.

Park did the news circuit. He caught postnews phone tips. A Tacoma psychic said Polly's body would be found near water. It was classic phony-psychic horseshit. Everyplace was near water one way or another. If they found her in a house in the high desert the psychic would take credit for guessing the faucet leaked.

Park pulled police reports. He looked for white men with children. He checked 911 calls. He found something that felt like something. A man who had been buying lottery tickets at some Sun Valley gas station reporting a standoff, knife versus gun. A man with a gun, a girl about Polly's age with him. Another man with a knife, shaved head, tattoos.

A blue thunderbolt tattoo, in fact. Prison ink. Aryan Steel used blue thunderbolts to mark their members. One for each kill they committed for the club. The buzz upped itself. The buzz pointed Park this way. Nate was Aryan Steel connected through his brother. Maybe he was trying to get out of state on the white-boy underground railroad. Maybe he just wanted a favor.

It wasn't a full-on buzz. But it was something. So he'd gone out to Antelope Valley. The woman behind the counter was the one who'd been working that day. Carla Knox, the sort of big hard woman that gets called a battle-ax by men who are scared of her. She'd clocked him as a cop the moment he walked through the door of the store. Park didn't try to look like a cop, but he knew the world you live in every day stains you whether you like it or not.

He badged her anyway. Her eyes went wider. The buzz kicked up in Park. He told it to settle down. Folk had all sorts of reasons for the cops to worry them. Maybe she had a baggie of something worth jail time in her pocket. Maybe she'd had a bad experience way back. Maybe she was just one of those people so soaked in guilt they see a cop and assume they're going to jail, that they're guilty of something, of everything.

Or maybe she knew something.

"Detective John Park," he said, and watched her throat go spastic.

Maybe she knew something.

He talked to her, barely listening to her answers, watching her body, the way her breath went in and out. He didn't need to listen to her, because he knew from the moment she opened her mouth it was horseshit. She was lying, that much was clear. The question was why?

His phone vibrated against his leg. He ignored it. He circled around for the kill. He leaned forward. He gave her the *you're-fucked* smile.

The phone started twitching again. He pulled out the phone. Saw it was from the precinct. He stepped away from Carla. He let the moment with Carla die.

"This better be good."

"It's Miller." The Major Crimes officer he shared a desk with. "I got a call for you. Want me to patch it through?"

"Take a fucking message."

"It's a little girl. Says her name is Polly McClusky. Says she wants to talk to you."

Chest pains told Park he'd stopped breathing. He felt skin tingles. He wondered if this was what junkies felt like just before the OD sucked them under. He walked out of the store without even a look back to see Carla's face.

9

NATE

—

FONTANA

Just don't lie and say it's about the girl.

Magic's house was right where Jake said it was. Nate sat in the dark in front of it. He did a pre-murder checklist. Means. Method. Escape route. Justification. That last part was easy. He just couldn't lie to himself and say it was for the girl. This was something for him, something to make himself feel whole, or if not whole then at least patched. He couldn't go on, do the things he had to do, knowing Magic was walking around having done what he did.

The girl back at the motel needed him. He swore he would die to protect her. But all the same, this had to be done. Sure as gravity.

Gray teevee light flickered from the front window. The house belonged to Chad Davidson, a man known as Magic. Nate had heard the name, late night in Susanville when the myths got spread. Magic had a cousin who'd died for the Steel in the Agua

Dulce shoot-out. Agua Dulce was legendary. The OK Corral starring white power killers and meth heads. Some suckmouth marked for death took on a truckload of Steel killers in the middle of the high desert. It ended in a cattle stampede and wildfire. Magic's cousin Carter caught a buckshot load in the face. Nobody ever found the suckmouth. Magic needed payback. Magic found the suckmouth's old biker gang. Magic took thumbs as trophies. Can't ride a chopper with no thumbs. Magic left a bunch of half-handed bastards pawning their bikes.

Magic had got his vengeance. And maybe he thought he'd done it for his brother found half-headed and burned in the desert, but Nate knew he had not. He knew that vengeance was a dumb and selfish act, and he knew if it went wrong he would leave Polly exposed and alone. Nate would be a fuckup again, one last, worst time.

But he was going to do it anyway. The ghost of his brother inside his head would have it no other way.

NATE HAD BEEN HERE an hour already. He knew Magic was inside. But he had a woman with him. They might be in there all night. But Nate doubted it. Magic didn't seem the type to cuddle after. So he waited.

He knew Magic was just the triggerman. Crazy Craig Hollington was the one who'd killed Avis and Tom. He was the one who put the greenlight on all of them. He was the only one who could lift it.

So kill him too, the ghost of his brother hooted in his head. Easy for the dead to say. Crazy Craig was untouchable. He was locked down in Supermax. The guards said it was to protect the world from Crazy Craig. Nate wondered if the hacks were dumb enough to believe that. Being locked in the room with no view didn't stop Crazy Craig. Ask Avis.

Don't lie and say it's for Avis either.

She wasn't his woman, not when she died, and she'd never really been his anyway—one thing Nate knew for sure was that nobody belonged to anybody but themselves, not in the end. But so what? Nate could know it was bullshit and still know he had to do it. He was powerless against the thing inside him, the thing with the voice of his brother that said this had to be done. And he was glad he was powerless against it. This was a thing he could do. He could kill Magic. He could avenge Avis, at least partway, whether it helped her or not. And then? Since he couldn't kill Crazy Craig, running was the only thing left. He guessed he and Polly would make like the suckmouth from the Agua Dulce shootout. Disappear. They could find someplace where Aryan Steel couldn't touch them. South, down in Mexico. He'd heard whispers of a place called Perdido, down at the tip of Baja, a place you could stay forever.

Don't lie and say it's about the girl.

He couldn't keep her. He was already poisoning her. Polly thought he hadn't known she'd been there when he'd put Jake in the fire. He'd seen her, though, right as he'd put his knee on Jake's belly and pressed him into the coals. He'd seen her eyes wild and alive watching his violence. He understood how she felt. It scared him all the more because he understood it, because it was the surest he'd ever been that she was his.

The door to the house opened. The featherwood walked out. She had combat boots. She had the featherwood 'do—a skull shaved down to fuzz everywhere but her bangs, which hung in her face. She had black fingernails. She had crank jitters you could spot in the dark.

He waited for her to get into her truck and drive away. Her brake lights lit up and the time was here and Nate felt his strength leave him.

You got to feel weak to get strong. Nick said that, in the car outside what was to be Nate's first liquor store. When he saw Nate's hands shaking. *You got to feel weak to get strong. Don't run away from it.*

Nate closed his eyes. Took deep breaths the way Nick had taught him. Breathing was how you talked to the animal in you, Nick had taught him. Nick had talked to his animal a lot, and it had talked to him, and Nick had taught Nate about it, and now here he was. He opened the car door and slipped out into the night.

NATE KNOCKED LIGHT on the door, the way the woman would knock if she was coming back because she'd forgotten something.

His blood like shook soda in his veins.

He heard a man walk to the other side of the door. Nate swore he could see the man through the wood. Could feel him somehow lean against the door to peek out the eyehole.

One more breath. In and out.

He kicked the door. The door popped open. The door popped Magic in his face. Nate walked in. He got the pistol raised. Time slowed down.

Magic had an old-school Mohawk. He had an iron cross on the bare scalp above his right ear. He had a dotted line tattoo across his throat that said CUT HERE. His nose was a red smear from where the door had tagged him. Magic had four blue bolts on his arm. The bottom two were wet. Fresh.

Two fresh bolts for two new kills. One was Avis, the other her man. Nate's brain took the time to have that thought. That was a mistake. Thoughts moved too slow for fighting.

Magic's boot came up kicking. It moved slow, like the air was syrup. But time was fucked now and Nate was moving slow too. The boot crashed into his knee. Nate went down.

Magic came on top of him, his eyes murder hot. He talked. The world moved too slow for Nate to decode the sounds.

Magic got his hands around Nate's throat about the time Nate noticed he didn't have the gun anymore. Magic squeezed. Nate could still take sips of air. His vision didn't blur at the edges. The volume of the world stayed the same. Magic didn't know shit about chokes.

Nate broke Magic's grip. Magic fell on top of him. Magic felt Nate's face. He fumbled for Nate's eyes. Nate hugged him close. He pressed Magic's face into his chest. Magic bit through Nate's shirt. He broke skin. Nate rode the pain. He got a knee under Magic's stomach. Nate kicked out, flipped the man over, landed on top. Magic kept searching for Nate's eyes. Nate grabbed a wrist. He twisted it. Heard a pop. Heard a scream. Kept twisting. Magic rodeo-bucked him, knocked him off balance. Magic reached for something on the ground with his good arm. Nate saw the gun come up at him just in time to think *oh shit—*

10

PARK

—

ANTELOPE VALLEY

Park started the car. The radio blared loud rock. He twisted the knob till it went away. He fired up headlights. He held the phone against his ear with his shoulder. He listened to clicks and pops on the phone. He prayed Miller had finally learned how to transfer a goddamn call.

High-pitched whistling on the other end of the phone. Like a kid breathing through snot rockets.

Could be a prank call. Could be a loony. Could be Polly.

"This is Detective Park."

Don't be a prank call. Don't be a loony.

"Hello?" He waited for an answer. Nothing but whistling, then a girl's voice.

"Hi."

"Polly? Are you Polly McClusky?"

"Yeah."

It was her. The buzz told him so. The fear in her voice goosed him. All the sudden it wasn't about the buzz anymore. Or anyway there was something real behind it. The fear in the little girl's voice. Depth charges boomed in his chest. He put the car in gear. The car spit gravel as it pulled out of the lot. He pointed the car back toward the highway.

"Is your father with you?"

"He's not here. He's coming back."

"Where are you?"

"Can you help me?"

"That's what I want to do."

The whistling double-timed.

"I know." The voice so tiny.

"What do you know, Polly?"

"She's dead. They murdered her. Her and Tom too."

"They? Who is they?"

"I'm scared," she said.

"You don't have to be. Tell me where you are."

"Please don't hurt him." Something had broken in the girl now and she sobbed as she talked. "I just don't want to be here anymore. But don't hurt him please."

"Polly, you called me. I can help you. But you've got to tell me where you are."

Seconds passed. He knew not to press. He drummed on the steering wheel, *come on come on come on.*

"The Scenic Heights. It's a motel. Room 23."

Eureka bingo bull's-eye.

"Polly, I want you to know you're going to be safe."

A moment of nothing but whistles. Park drove fast. The poppies a smear on the edge of his eyes.

"Oh no." Her voice a ragged little whisper.

"Polly, don't hang—"

"Someone's coming," she said right before the phone went dead in Park's ear.

11

POLLY

—

MOUNT VERNON / THE BARSTOW FREEWAY

Polly hung up the phone quiet as she could. Through the dark she thought she could see the doorknob flutter. Shadows rolled behind the blinds. From the other side of the door came the sound of the key scraping around the lock, hunting, the way mom and Tom would do it when they came back from bar nights. Polly put her hand on the bat, her other on the bear. The door swung open. With the outside lights behind the man he looked like nothing but a shadow.

"Polly . . . Polly, you there?"

The shape took a step. Her dad stumbled bad, caught himself on the table. Polly saw his red hand in a shaft of light. Red smears on the table. His pant leg was soaked. Red on black. A dark hole near the top of his thigh that yawned as he moved. Polly felt her insides flop. She wanted to run to him. She wanted to run away from him. She didn't do either.

They rode in a different car than before, a black thing that looked like it went fast with chips and dents all over. Sirens rose and fell in the distance. A helicopter stirred the air someplace overhead. Were they coming for them? Were they following them?

Had she made them come?

She'd called the help number not knowing what she wanted. She only knew this was too big for her, something she couldn't handle. She'd called because she needed help. She knew it meant her dad would probably go back to jail, no matter what Detective Park had said. But now he was hurt, hurt bad, and looking at him bleeding made Polly feel like she stood at the edge of a cliff with her toes poking over and a wind blowing against her back.

She couldn't lose him, she saw that now. He was all she had and so he was all that mattered. And maybe she was all he had anymore, and maybe that meant she mattered.

HE DROVE SITTING STRAIGHT UP. He kept his hoodie in his lap to keep the hole in his leg out of sight. He was so focused on driving he didn't even look at the police car rolling past them the other way. Polly wondered if it was heading back to the motel. She pushed that thing down. There were bigger things to worry about now. Sooner things.

"Do you know where the hospital is?" she asked.

"Not going to a hospital," he said.

"Please. Please, please go to a doctor," she said, the jagged things inside her coming out in her voice.

"You go to a doctor with a bullet in you, the doctor has to call the cops," he said. "That's law. And I can't have the cops on me. Cops get me and it's over. For both of us."

The word *cops* wrote itself in fire across her mind, even before she made sense of the word *bullet*.

"People die from bullets," she said.

"If I go to jail, I'll die for sure," he said. "The same ones who . . . the same ones who got your mom. The blue lightning guys. They're in there waiting for me."

Something went over his face like a wave. Pain or something worse.

"They hurt you?"

"It was the one," he said. "The one who got your mom. But I got him."

They came to one of the big truck stops with twenty pumps, a diner, showers, a gift shop. On one side of the lot sat a double-wide, TRUCKER MINISTRIES stenciled down the side of it.

Her dad pulled into a parking spot far away from the glow of the truck stop. He parked in the shadows of the overnight lot, semi trucks with dark cabs.

"You need to go in there," he said. "Find the first aid shelf. Get lots of gauze and bandages. Hydrogen peroxide. Disinfectant. Hand sanitizer. A pair of sweatpants if you can find some. You're gonna fix me up."

She shook her head *no* so fierce she heard things wiggle in her skull. She couldn't help with a bullet, not a bullet inside a person. Didn't he know she was just a kid? Couldn't he see she was from Venus?

"Polly," he said again. "I can't, not without you. You understand?"

He shifted over onto his hip to reach his back pocket. She heard his teeth grind, watched muscles in his face twitch. She saw his hand fish for his wallet. She made a decision. She let herself speak.

"No," Polly said, louder than she meant. Her dad looked to her.

"You'll get blood on it," Polly said. "Let me."

"Smart girl," he said. He nodded at his back pocket like *go ahead then*. She plucked out the wallet and opened it. She pulled out a twenty.

"Take another," he said. "Just in case."

When she had, she stuck the wallet in the console. She opened the door. The overhead light came on. She saw her dad pale and sweat-slicked. He squinted against the sudden light.

THE PLASTIC BAGS bounced against Polly's legs as she walked back from the store slow and calm, the way her dad had driven. She looked up to see a night full of stars. Most of the time in the Empire the stars were hidden. They were out far enough for hundreds of stars. Polly knew they were millions of miles away, so far away they might be dead already and the light was just the past catching up with Earth. Polly wondered if there really were other planets out there where everything was like it was here, but a little different. She wondered if there was any world at all where she came out okay.

When she opened the car door the overhead light came on. Her dad's face had turned into fishbelly and his eyes were closed.

"Daddy?"

His head turned slow. His eyes peeled back like it was work to do it.

"Haven't heard you call me that since you was little."

"I got the stuff." She held up the plastic bag.

"This ain't going to work," he said. He opened his hands like *look around*.

She looked in the backseat. It was small, the way the backseats of fast cars often were. There was no way she and her dad could fit back there.

"We got to go back to the motel," he said. She saw flashes of policemen in the dark with eyes like wolves under their blue hats. She pushed the thought down. She scanned the parking lot. She saw the trucker church.

"How about there?" she asked.

She thought he'd tell her no, he was the boss, but he didn't. He nodded and said *okay*. Polly felt something shift between them, that maybe she was a little bigger in his eyes. And maybe, to tell it true, he was a little smaller in hers. But still huge.

THE DOOR TO THE DOUBLE-WIDE was thin sheet metal, SINNERS WELCOME stenciled across it in fading paint. Polly got out and walked up the metal steps to the trailer's door.

"Shit," her dad said. "I'm gonna have to jimmy it."

"Nuh-uh," she said.

She tried the door. It came open.

"Tom told me about them once. They leave them open," she said, "so people can pray in them whenever."

Polly turned on the light. Wood paneling, a podium, three rows of chairs. Shag carpet. A framed picture of the friendly kind of Jesus hung over the altar.

Her dad came up the stairs. He laid himself out next to the altar, using one of the chairs to help himself down. He unbuckled his jeans.

"My shoes," he said. Polly didn't move.

"Polly," he said again. She went to his feet and unlaced his sneakers. First she pulled the shoe off his left leg, the unhurt one. She yanked his right shoe. His leg shuddered. She saw his throat muscles do funny things. She felt her throat muscles do funny things too. She fumbled with the shoe for a better grip. A sound came out of her dad's throat that made her let go. The shoe stayed on.

"Goddamn it," her dad said. "Don't worry about me. Just one clean yank."

A memory from deep down, from when memories were new, bubbled up to the top of her head. A loose tooth in her mouth, twisting in its socket, her first impermanence. His rough fingers in her mouth, a count to three and a dull snap of pain that reached up into her skull. The tooth in his hand. Red-tipped. How he'd shown it to her and smiled.

"Brave girl," he'd said as he pressed her skull-fresh tooth into her palm. Where had that memory been living? When had she ever been brave?

She dug her fingers into the mouth of the shoe like he'd once done with her head. She yanked hard. She fell back with the shoe in her hands. His sock poked out his pant leg, soaked plum almost to the toe. She looked up at him. He had a weird smile on his face.

"What?" she asked.

"Nothing," he said. "Good girl."

She felt something like time overlapping itself, him standing there with her baby tooth in his hand, her standing here now with his bloody sneaker in hers. That same weird smile on his face both times.

Brave girl.

She warmed to her work. She got the first aid stuff ready while he got himself out of his jeans. When she turned back to him he'd wrapped himself in the blanket from the back of the car. Only his bare bloody leg stuck out. She made herself look at it. The wound on the side of his leg gaped. It looked like a crater of skin, a center of meat weeping red.

Her stomach went sour. Her hands shook too bad to unscrew the lid to the hydrogen peroxide.

"Breathe," he said. "Close your eyes. Breathe deep. In through the nose," he said. "Out through the mouth. Loud enough that I can hear it."

She did it. In, out. In, out. She opened her eyes. She looked down at her hands. They still shook. But less. She unscrewed the bottle. She hunched next to his leg. She put her left hand on his leg. He was hot to the touch.

She poured hydrogen peroxide into the wound. It fizzed pink. It made her think of grapefruit soda. Part of her wanted to laugh and laugh and never stop. She let it pass through her. She breathed like he'd taught her.

"What about the bullet?" she asked.

"What about it?"

"Don't we have to get it out?"

"Naw," he said. "It's done all the bad it's going to do. We're just gonna leave it be."

She took a bottle of hand sanitizer and squirted it onto her hands.

"Your mom ever make you go to church?" he asked, maybe just because the silence was broken now.

She followed his eyes to the picture of Jesus. She shook her head like *no*.

"In first grade one time, Ms. Groger had us do a drawing of our family at Christmastime. I didn't want to do it. I just didn't want to. So I told her I was Jewish."

She spread some disinfectant goo from a tube onto her fingertips.

"You did what now?"

She dabbed her finger onto the hole in his leg, so gently.

"Told her I was Jewish. Said we didn't celebrate Christmas. So I wouldn't have to do the stupid drawing."

She spread disinfectant on a gauze pad.

She pressed it into the wound. His fists balled up in the folds of the blanket.

"So she didn't make me do the drawing. But what she did was she called Mom."

Polly swallowed something sharp before going on.

"She called Mom, and she told Mom what happened, and she said, 'I'm so sorry, I didn't know you were Jewish,' and Mom said 'Well, hell, neither did I!'"

"Sounds like her all right," her dad said.

Polly missed her again fresh, fresh as the hole in his leg. But she smiled at the memory, and the crying wasn't so bad that she couldn't finish the story.

"So what she did was, she said if I wanted to be Jewish I could be, and she took me to that temple over in Ontario. And it was kind of cool, they had this real old book and they read from it, but for real it was as boring as regular church. So I decided I wasn't Jewish and I wasn't anything. And Mom said that it was good I tried."

She ran her tongue over her tooth, the one that had grown in the place of the one he'd yanked. Some things get replaced, she thought, and some things never will. She put a bandage over the gauze and started wrapping it. After a while the tears stopped.

"Make it tighter," he said. She did it again. She taped the bandage to itself and sat back. She shook the numb feeling out of her fingertips.

"Is it okay?" Polly asked. He leaned forward and looked at her work.

"That'll do," he said. He took her by the arm and squeezed it. "That'll do just fine."

They sat there like that for a little while, and it was quiet for Polly, even on the inside.

12

NATE

—

THE BARSTOW FREEWAY

Nick had taught him about bullet wounds a long time ago. Yanking bullets out was movie bullshit. You'd do more damage pulling it out than leaving it alone. Nick told him a story he'd heard in lockup, about three stickup artists in L.A. One caught a bullet in the shoulder and was bleeding bad, like heading-for-death bad. They didn't want to take him to a hospital with a gunshot wound in him, so what they did was set a badass pit bull on the man's shoulder. The dog chewed the bullet wound to hamburger and they took him to the hospital as the victim of a dog attack. Moral of the story, Nick said, was don't get shot.

If it didn't kill you straightaway, and you didn't bleed out, the worst thing about a bullet in you was the things it carried with it. A bullet, hot from the barrel, was cleaned by the fire that launched it, but when it hits you, it gathers up bits of your clothes, your skin, and sucks them inside you, along for the ride. If the bullet or the bleeding didn't kill you, it was those little bits of jeans and skin that you had to worry about. They led to infection. But the girl had cleaned the wound well. All he could do was watch for the purple to spread, and worry about what to do about it when it did.

NATE CHECKED THE SWEATPANTS the girl had bought him as he limped across the truck stop lot. No blood spots. There was pain and he limped pretty bad, but that couldn't be helped. At least the bullet had missed the bone.

In the truck stop he bought a pint of whiskey and a stack of beach towels. He found Polly waiting for him at the car. They laid the towels over the bloody car seats. Nate broke the seal on the bottle and had a long drink. It burned clean inside him. Like a bullet from the barrel. He chased it with bottled water. He realized he was parched. He drained it dry. When it was empty he crunched the plastic bottle in his hand. The crunch of it shook him. It coughed up gunshot replays in his head.

HE'D HAD MAGIC in his hands when Magic got hold of the pistol. The flash and bang from the barrel turned the world psychedelic. Darklights blossomed in Nate's eyes. High whines in his ears. Nate got his hand on the barrel. Ignored the hot metal burning his hands. He twisted the barrel. He felt Magic's finger bones snap in the trigger guard. He pulled the gun out of Magic's twisted fingers. He reared back. He got a fastball grip on the pistol. He dented the iron cross on the side of Magic's skull. He did it again. The man's eyes went null. Nate put the barrel in between Magic's slack lips. He saw a condor in a clear blue sky. He pulled the trigger. Magic laid a fan of slop on the rug behind him.

The corpse summoned a moment of clarity for Nate. How dumb it had all been. How close he'd come to losing it all, dooming Polly. The corpse solved nothing. Polly was still in danger. So was Nate. Crazy Craig had a dozen killers just like Magic. Aryan Steel had killers anywhere he could think to run. He'd risked everything for the ghost of his brother.

He lay back on the dead man's legs. He looked up at the ceiling, tried to catch his breath. The world went soft at the edges, like Magic's choke had finally started working. Nate felt something warm, wet on his leg. That's how he realized he'd been shot.

"Are you okay?"

The girl's words brought him back. He nodded. He leaned forward to key the ignition. A wave of pain came over him, knocking him back into the car seat.

"Goddamn," he said. He wrestled with the pain until he got a hold of it, held it down.

Polly moved the bear so it looked like he was climbing his seat. The bear cocked his head so it looked at Nate. Placed a paw on his forehead, checking for a temperature. The bear looked back to Polly and nodded. She caught Nate looking at her. She looked at him like he might reach out and smack her.

"I know he's not real," she said. "You know I know, right?"

"I do now," he said.

He held out his fist to the bear. The bear reached out with his paw and gave him a fist bump. He thought he might have got a smile out of Polly but he didn't. Nate sank back into his seat. The whiskey took hold of him. He knew if he drank much more he might have a hard time making it back to the motel. He needed sleep. Needed to have nothing at all for as many hours as life could give him.

"Think I'm good to go back," Nate said. "You ready?"

"The motel?" Her face made Nate think of rabbits when the owls screech.

"One more night," he said. "Then we're moving on."

"Yeah," Polly said. The way she said it made him look at her. But her face was pressed against the window and he couldn't see whatever it was that made him look.

13

POLLY

—

FONTANA / MOUNT VERNON

Polly and her dad rolled past the auto track. That put them minutes away from the motel. She wished she could reach back in time to stop herself from calling for help. She pressed her face against the window. The cool of it let her know she was burning.

"We'll sleep late," he said. "Then we'll go to L.A. in the morning."

He put a hand on the top of her head, rough fingers against her scalp. A wave of acid crested at the back of her throat.

"Stop," she said. "Stop the car, stop it, stop it please."

"We're two minutes from the motel. Just hold the fuck on."

She felt whales roll inside her stomach.

"Stop the car, stop the car!"

"Polly—"

A noise came from deep inside her, a burp and a moan all in one. She got the window down. She dumped her stomach out into the night. She painted the side of the car nacho-cheese orange.

She fell back into her seat. Tears and snot and sick cooled on her face.

"Don't go back to the motel," she said through tears. "You can't go back. Please don't go back. Please. Please don't make me tell you why."

He turned the car onto a side street and parked on a dark spot of the road. He turned off the headlights. She wiped her face on her shirt. She fought for her breath.

"Now you listen to me," he said. "If there's something I need to know, you got to tell me."

The confession came out of her the same speed her dinner had.

"I called the police. While you were gone. There's a policeman and he said he could help and I didn't know what to do. I'm sorry. I don't want you to go away again. I don't want to be alone. I just got scared. Please, I'm sorry."

He wiped his face with his hands. He pressed his palms into his eyes. He kept them there while he talked.

"I don't know what I'm doing either," he said. "Hell, a week ago I got told when to sleep and when to eat and when to piss. And now I've got the whole world in front of me with no map, and the only little part of it that don't feel like it's trying to kill me is you and that damn bear."

He took his hands off his eyes and looked at her. She held his gaze, though it made her heart beat all the way down to the roots of her teeth.

"I never gave you a choice. You're just a kid, but even a kid has to have a choice. So here it is. You want, I'll let you off a block from the motel. You find the policeman, you tell them to keep you safe. Hell, maybe they can."

She opened her mouth to answer. He shushed her with his hand.

"The other choice is you come with me. It could get scary. Even dangerous. But if you're with me . . . well, at least you'll be with me, and I'll do what I can. And going with the cops, it might not be safe either. There's folk who want us dead. And they're not going to stop. Could be they could get to you in a group home, or juvenile, or even out on the street.

"If it was up to me, you'd come along with me. We'll get out of here for a while. Head over to L.A. Then we do something to make ourselves safe. I don't want it to be up to me if you come or not. I want it to be up to you. So you got to choose."

She felt every inch of skin all over her body at once. She nodded like *yes*. Then she felt like that wasn't good enough. For a thing like this you had to say it. So she did.

"I want to stay with you."

He turned his face away from her. When he talked, his voice was rough and low.

"Well all right then."

He put the car in gear. He pulled a U-turn. They headed west.

14

PARK

—

MOUNT VERNON / ANTELOPE VALLEY

Park drove to Carla's house cop-fast. Passing headlights threw up weird shapes in his eyes. He saw the little girl in the shapes. The one who had called him. The one he'd let down.

He'd missed her. He wouldn't miss again.

Park hit the apartment complex at speed. He stomped brakes, tires squealed. He left the car in the fire zone, fuck-you-I'm-a-cop style. He double-timed the stairs to Carla's apartment. *Bam bam bam* on the door, fuck-you-I'm-a-cop style.

Carla had sleep boogers and terror in her eyes.

"Detective—"

"Invite me in," Park said. Cops were like vampires that way. They had to be invited in. She stepped aside. He came in. Her house was chaos. Everything was chaos right now.

"You got a brother in Chino," he said.

"What's he got to do with this?"

"Nothing at all," Park said, "except I can touch him, and that's how I'm going to touch you."

"Is that blood?" she asked. Park looked down on his shirt. Blood spatter from when Park had broken the john's nose at the motel. The one he thought was Nate McClusky.

"Yeah," he said to Carla. Saw the fear jolt in her. It jolted him back. The thing in his brain whispered *chase it*. He picked up a beer bottle from the table. He thought about the little girl. How scared she'd sounded. He threw the bottle against the wall. There was only a part of him that felt bad when Carla screamed.

THEY'D BEEN CAMPED OUT at the motel for three hours when they caught the guy creeping in the bushes. When a uni radioed that a white guy had just crawled out the back window of one of the units, Park ran from his hiding spot. He hit the guy elbow first. He heard a crunch like celery snapping. He turned the guy over already knowing from the guy's soft body that he wasn't Nate. Just some dumb son of a bitch who had himself a fifty-dollar hooker in his room and saw one of the unis, thought it was a bust and went out the back window.

Pretty soon after that Park knew it was a dead end. He called off the stakeout. They grabbed the manager and went into Nate's motel room. They found luggage. They found fast food bags in the trash. Park left a plainclothes to sit on the place in case they came back. But Park knew they'd missed them.

He should have gone home from there. He should have gone to sleep. He didn't. The woman from the gas station had known something. He radioed in for Carla's home address. He chewed nails while he drove to her.

"Your brother," he said once he'd given the apartment a once-over. "He's an Aryan Steel wannabe up in Chino."

"What's he got to do with it?"

"I did a favor once," Park said. "Guy named Joker. He runs Chino for La Eme. Now I know white people are used to running shit, so maybe you don't know. In California the whiteboys are outnumbered six to one. Aryan Steel takes a backseat to La Eme. So if I call in my chit with Joker and tomorrow your brother is bunking with the carnales, it's not gonna go well for him."

Carla moaned.

"Nate McClusky," he said. "You saw him. You saw his daughter."

Carla nodded *yes*. She was scared preverbal.

"You ever live in Fontana, Carla?"

She nodded *yes*.

"You knew Nate from there?"

Yes.

"He was there to see you, wasn't he?"

Yes.

"He was there with one of his buddies from lockup."

No.

"The guy he fought with, he didn't come with him?"

No. Something pinned behind her eyes. Something she had her jaw latched shut to keep inside her. Something clawing and biting to get out.

"Tell me," he said, and watched her unlock.

"I sold Nate out. They were going to hurt my brother if I didn't."

"Who?"

"The Steel. They're the ones who killed Avis and her husband."

Park laughed, jagged, scaring Carla, scaring himself.

"Nate McClusky killed Avis and Tom Huff."

Carla shook her head *no*.

"Guy walks out of jail, kidnaps his daughter, the wife winds up dead and you want me to think he didn't kill her?"

She nodded *that's right*.

"Use your words, Carla."

"He took Polly 'cause he knew Avis was dead already. And Polly was next. He saved her life, you stupid son of a bitch."

Goddamn it.

He believed her.

That fucked up everything.

15

POLLY

—

POMONA

Lighter than blood, darker than pink. She chose the color herself. Her dad had wanted her to choose something dull, something brown. But she'd stood her ground. She wanted the red. After a while he'd nodded. "It'll make you different enough, I guess," he said.

It'll make you different. That's what she wanted.

She put the jar of dye on the bathroom counter of the new hotel room. She picked up the scissors from next to the jar of dye. She took a fistful of dirty-blond hair in her left hand. The scissors *chawed* through the hank of hair. She heard the noise as much through her skull as through her ears. She dumped the fistful of shorn hair into the trash. She grabbed a second chunk. She stopped. Her eyes tear-blurred. She let the tears come. They weren't sad, not this time. She couldn't say just what they were. After a while the tears stopped. She started cutting again. When she was done with that, she rinsed her hair in the sink. The cold water stinging against her scalp told her how alive she was.

She took some Vaseline and put a thin layer around her hairline. She put on the thin plastic gloves that came with the dye. She poured the red dye into her palms. She worked it into her hair. She wanted to look at herself in the mirror, but she didn't yet. She counted seconds as the dye set in. Then she ran the shower until the water was luke. She stuck her head under it. The water ran red and then it ran pink and then it ran clear.

She buried her head in a towel. She scrubbed, not just her hair, but her face too, the towel scratching, pressing it into the sockets of her eyes until she saw color galaxies be born and die in the dark behind her eyelids.

She dropped the towel to the floor. She turned to the mirror. Her hair hung in chunks to the side of her head. It was the color of watermelon meat. It played against her eyes, bringing them out. Her face looked different now, something there now that hadn't been there before, or maybe something that used to be there was gone. Her eyes seemed larger, or deeper, or something else, something more. She stared into them for a long time.

Gunfighter eyes, no lie.

PART II

. . . AND CUB

—

LOS ANGELES

16

NATE

—

LOS ANGELES

When you walk into a liquor store with a gun in your hand and a mask over your face, you rip the lid off the world. Time does real Einstein shit. It stretches; it shrinks.

One second through the door, before the first *oh shit oh shit oh shit* had passed through the clerk's head, Nate had time to remember the night Polly had been born. He'd gotten a call from Avis, fear in her voice. She told him she was in labor. The baby was coming. Would Nate be there? Would he meet her at the hospital?

And Nate said he'd be there. He'd hung up the phone. Looked over to Nick in the driver's seat. Nick had the pistol in his hand, his ski mask in his lap. He had that devil's smile.

"Everything cool?" Nick had asked. And Nate hadn't done a thing but nodded and slipped his own mask over his face.

THAT WHOLE MEMORY flashed through him in the time it took him to walk from the door to the counter. Nate waved the pistol at the clerk. The clerk fell back against the high-end booze behind him. Nate barked something slow-mo through the ski mask. The clerk moved. Nate figured the silent alarm had been triggered. It didn't matter either way. It would be over soon.

The clerk popped open the register. He dumped the cash drawer on the counter. The loose change spilled down onto the chip rack. The clerk babbled some liquid language from god knows where. It was an intimate moment, this moment between robber and victim. A gun to the head made you naked.

Nate put the gun to the man's head. He said, "Safe."

The clerk pushed aside the boner-pill display. The safe revealed itself. The clerk keyed in the combination. He got it wrong. He keyed it in again. He got it wrong. One more wrong guess locked the thing for twenty-four hours. Nate lowered the pistol.

"Take three deep breaths," he said.

The clerk gave him *what-the-fuck* eyes.

"I said take three deep breaths and then try it again."

The clerk followed instructions. In through the nose, out through the mouth times three. The clerk punched in the code.

Click.

The safe door rolled open. Nate eyeballed the inside. He did cash stack calculations in his head. He called it two large. Worth it.

You can't say that yet. Not until it's over.

The clerk bagged the cash. Nate took it. Headed for the door. Time corrected itself as he hit night air. He came back to the city in all its heat and ugliness. Like any drug, the stickup rush had a major downside. It couldn't last forever.

He got into the car, turned to Polly in the shotgun seat as he shifted into reverse. Her eyes glistened with life.

"That's how you do it," he said. She nodded. She smiled. Her smile scared him.

17

POLLY

—

NORTH HOLLYWOOD

When you stand in the hills over Los Angeles the world turns upside down. Above you the night sky is black dirt, and below you the million lights of the city glitter like a bowl full of stars. It felt right to Polly that they'd come to an upside-down world. She felt pretty upside down herself.

Polly ate a chiliburger and looked at the stars below while sitting on the hood of the green monster, which was what she'd named the car they'd bought when they'd gotten to Los Angeles and dumped Magic's car. It was the best chiliburger—maybe even the best food—she'd ever had. So good she made an *mmmm* when she took a big bite like somebody from a dumb commercial.

Her dad smiled and went back to counting the money in his lap.

"Tastes good, right?" he said. "Your uncle Nick said one time, stealing was the best sauce in the world. It's 'cause you're a little more alive than you used to be."

They'd just come from robbing a liquor store, which was a thought she could have only in an upside-down world. It seemed like stealing was a thing that should have bothered her. It didn't. It turned out she liked it. In these first days in L.A., Polly felt like she was meeting this girl for the first time, this girl with watermelon hair and gunfighter eyes.

Polly mock-fed the bear a dollop of chili. The bear waved farts away from his butt. The bear giggled silently. Her dad laughed through his own chiliburger. Polly and he laughed together, and it was like hearing a song she hadn't heard in a long time.

HE'D EXPLAINED EVERYTHING to her on the fifty-mile ride to Los Angeles. About how the blue-thunderbolt bad guys were called Aryan Steel. How they wanted to kill the two of them. How they'd killed her mom and Tom.

"There's only one thing I'm good at," he'd said as they'd driven in stop-and-go traffic into the behemoth of L.A. "That's robbing. Now Aryan Steel, they've got a lot of businesses. Lots of cash. What I'm going to do is keep robbing them and robbing them until they want a truce."

"Won't that just make them madder?"

"At first," he said. "But deep down, they're businessmen. If I cost them enough, they'll do whatever they can to stop me."

"Us," she said, looking down at the corpse of a coyote on the side of the road. If you drive on the highways all day, she thought, you see a lot of dead things.

"Huh?"

"We're going to rob them," she said. "I'm going to help. That was the deal."

They'd found the apartment a few days ago. An old Thai woman who was happy to have cash for the rent and no questions. Furnished, with two bedrooms, but they hardly ever used them. They slept on the couches in the living room, the teevee going all night. Her dad liked noise when he slept. It turned out she did too.

He woke in the morning and did his exercises. Polly and the bear watched. After, he sketched out what he knew about Aryan Steel. It turned into classes. Polly thought about school, her empty seat, if any of the kids missed her. Probably not, huh? But that was okay. She didn't miss them either. She had her own school now. He sketched on paper, how different gangs worked, how they fit together. He had worse handwriting than Polly. Polly took over the sketches. He talked to her about Aryan Steel.

"It's jail people who run things on the outside," he said.

"Why?"

"Because people on the outside come inside. All of them, once in a while, they all come inside. So sooner or later, the ones on the inside will get their hands on them."

He mapped the gangs down for her. Shot callers and associates. He had her put Crazy Craig at the top of the pyramid. He was the head. Below him, a couple of shot callers, lifers like him. One named Moonie, one named Despot. He told her about their tattoos, how they all told stories. There were the gangs with names like the Nazi Dope Boys and Peckerwood Nation. He told her how the gangs paid taxes to Aryan Steel. How it was all about money. She learned it all.

"There's lots of these folk in L.A.," he said. "We just got to find them."

"What are we looking for?"

"Dirty whiteboys," he said. "The kind that does business with the Steel. We need a thread to pull. We find where the dirty white-boys gather, we'll be able to find our way in."

"And then what?"

"We take the fight to them."

SHE WOKE THE DAY AFTER they'd robbed the liquor store to find him standing over her.

"Get up," he said. Something different in his voice, harder.

"What?"

"Up," he said. She got up.

"I want to see how many push-ups you can do."

"I'm not good at them."

"That's what doing them is for. To get better."

Her arms burned after just a couple. Her breath grew burrs, scraping her throat. Nate sat back. He watched her. She did five. On six her arms burned. She let her face touch the cool of the floor.

"One more," he said.

She pushed up with shaking arms. She made a noise. She did it. She rolled onto her back to look at him.

"You got to feel weak to get strong," he said.

"Huh?"

"Your uncle Nick used to say it. Means if you want your mus-cles to get strong, you got to push them until they're weak. It's like that for most things in life. If you feel strong all day, you're prob-ably not getting any stronger."

She nodded.

"Now you ready to start learning for real? You sure?"

To tell it true, she wasn't. She wanted to run and hide. She didn't want to feel weak even if it led to being strong. But the girl with watermelon hair couldn't hide.

"I'm sure," she said.

HE SHOVED FURNITURE AROUND so they had enough carpet to move on. He got down on the floor.

"We're going to start with chokes," he said. "There's two kinds of chokes. There's strangles and blood chokes. What's the two kind of chokes?"

"Strangles," she said, "and blood chokes."

"Strangles, you know that word *strangling*, right? It means can't breathe. Strangles are okay. They work all right. But do me a favor, hold your breath for as long as you can."

She breathed in, sealed her nose, let her cheeks puff out. He did the same. She felt like a balloon, like her butt was connected to the ground by a string and that was the only reason she didn't float away. Her dad's eyes bulged, like holding his breath was killing him, and Polly's breath burst out in a laugh.

"No fair," she said. She felt jumpy, something like a jagged sugar rush.

"You did pretty good," he said. "That's the problem with strangles. Air chokes, strangles, they take a long time to work. Now the other kind of choke is a blood choke."

He moved her around so his chest was against her back. She breathed in. The smell of him made her feel bulletproof.

He snaked his left hand under her chin so that his elbow cradled the center of her throat. His bicep pressed against the left side of her throat, his forearm against the right.

"You take the left hand, your choking arm, and you grab your right bicep. It's just for leverage," he said. "I'm going to choke you now. When you feel it, just tap my arm. What are you going to do?"

"Tap your arm," she said.

"Right. When you squeeze a choke, you squeeze with your whole body. Like this."

The arm around her throat tightened slowly, and his chest pressed into her back all at once. And there wasn't any pain or anything like that. It was just that the world started to get smaller and farther away. And it was only right before the world disappeared all the way that she understood what was happening. She tapped his arm. The pressure on her neck went away and the world came back.

"You okay?"

She nodded. At least maybe she did. She felt a stranger in her own body.

"Tap sooner than that. You don't need to go to sleep to see it works. Did it work?"

She nodded like *yeah*. So weird that nothingness was so close to her, always, and she'd never even known. She wondered what else she didn't know, and the sugar rush intensified.

"We're starting with chokes," he said, "because you're small. Chokes, you don't have to be big and strong. See, all you're doing is squeezing those two little arteries at the side of the neck that go up and feed the brain. And even a little girl like you is strong enough to squeeze them."

He turned around.

"Now you do it to me."

She moved behind him. She stood on her knees. He leaned back against her so she could get her arm around his neck.

"Start at the back of the jaw," he told her. "Under the ear. Move your hand all the way under my neck. Your arm will fit better."

She put her left hand to his jawline and moved her hand under his chin until her elbow hooked around his Adam's apple. Her face pressed into the fuzz at the back of his head. He hadn't shaved it in a while and the fuzz was soft when she put her cheek against it. It smelled like boy soap and sweat.

"Now grab your other bicep with that hand," he said. She did it.

"Your other hand, the one that's not under my neck, put it behind my head so the back of your hand is against my skull. And what you're going to do is, squeeze against the sides of my neck with the one arm and push against the back of my neck with the other. Squeeze it from all sides. Like a snake."

"Okay."

"Now squeeze," he said.

She squeezed.

"With your body too," he said, his voice thin. She leaned her chest into his back, felt her whole body as a single thing, like a snake, she thought, and she squeezed and he tapped her arm, two sharp taps. She let go. He leaned forward. He coughed. When he turned to her she could see his eyes were watery.

"You did it," he said.

"I did? For real?"

"For real," he said.

She felt something strange, a thrumming in her muscles, a thrumming in her mind. It took her a second to find the word for what she felt. It was a word she hadn't got to use for herself in a long time. The word was *power*.

"Show me more," she said. He nodded like *hell yes*.

18

POLLY

—

HUNTINGTON BEACH

It wasn't until they'd been training and hunting for two weeks that they reached the ocean, and their prey. One moment they were in the never-ending sprawl of the city—Polly had already been in L.A. long enough to feel like the sprawl went on forever—then the road they were on ended at a T, and beyond, a great blue darkness stretching out forever. Polly never would have thought something so big could come without warning.

They walked toward the roar of the ocean. Polly took off her shoes at the edge of the sand. They stopped at a fruit cart and bought fruit bowls. Melons and papayas and mangoes. The woman squeezed a lime over the bowl, and salt and chili pepper too.

"*Gracias,*" Polly said. The bear blew the woman a kiss. The woman laughed.

Overhead, gulls did lazy circles. A group of girls walked by in bathing suits. Her dad watched them.

"Bathing suits didn't used to look like that," he said, and Polly

didn't know who he was saying it to but it sure wasn't her. She put
a piece of mango to the bear's snout. It waved a paw over its snout
like *hot chili pepper*.

Polly walked with her head up. When they first got to L.A.
Polly had been worried about being recognized. She knew the
police were still looking for her and her dad. Then one day she
saw her face on a billboard. It wasn't like the time she saw herself
on the news. It was like a stranger looking back. She stood right
under it without fear, people passing and not knowing it was her.
She looked up at her dad with his beard and fuzzy head and sunglasses. She knew then she was safe from being seen.

They reached the wet sand. They padded to where the water
could lick the sand from between their toes. Sea foam glided
across the wet sand. It hugged its way around her foot. Colder
than she ever thought it would be. The water sucked sand with it
as it fled back to the ocean. She liked the feeling of it, the sharp air
and cold water and rough sand.

She looked up at her dad, found him staring down the beach
again. Probably more girls, she thought. But then she saw them. A
group of men and women drinking beer in cans. The men in cutoff jeans, the girls in tiny T-shirts. The men had tattoos, mostly
dark blue, scribbly, like the ones all over her dad.

Young bodies, hard eyes.

She gave her dad a look like *them?*

"Yeah," he said.

THEY WAITED FOR the party to wrap up. Polly watched them side-eyed.
It seemed like the way a spy would do it, or a ninja.

Her dad wasn't as sneaky as she was. He took peeks. He
watched one of them in particular. A woman. Her hair was cut

boy short, with long bangs that that flopped over her forehead. She had green eyes too big for her face. She didn't wear a swimsuit, just cutoffs and a T-shirt, tight so it showed off her boobs. And she was with the group, but she wasn't really with them. She was just outside the circle, and she sat with her body facing a bit away from everybody else. Polly was good at noticing stuff like that. She wondered if that's why her dad was looking at her. Or maybe it was just her boobs. The thought gave Polly a feeling she didn't like. She had to hunt for the word. *Doom.* Doom was the word.

Beach cops walked by. The air changed. The party got quiet. Next to her, Polly felt her dad go still. He pulled down the sleeves on his shirt to make sure the ink was covered. He ran a hand over the week's worth of fuzz on his head and face.

"We're not doing anything," Polly said.

"The one thing I'm scared of," he said, "is being locked up again. Out here I can fight. I can keep you safe. Inside it's all over."

"They don't recognize us."

"Just takes one is all," he said. "And everything goes to shit."

The people they were watching seemed like they felt the same way. Even when the cops walked on their moods had soured. The group broke up, headed up the sand toward the parking lot.

"Who do we follow?" she asked.

"Her," he said, pointing to the dark-haired girl. The one Polly knew he was going to pick.

"Why?" Polly said. "Don't we want one of the tough guys?"

"We're hunting," he said. "When you hunt and you find a pack, you got to find the loner. The weak one. The one you can split off the fold. She's the one. We stick with her."

It made sense to Polly. After all, Polly had noticed that the girl was an outsider too. It was even scientific choosing her, the way he said it. So why did it sound like a lie?

19

NATE

—

NORTH HOLLYWOOD

The next morning he taught her how to take a punch.

"Today is going to be hard," Nate said to her as she sat across from him, sheened with sweat from their warmup. He was talking to himself as much as Polly. He tried to say it calm and easy. He remembered the day when he'd been the one on the receiving end of this.

"Are we going to watch that woman today?" she asked. They'd followed her—the woman with the green eyes that struck Nate right at the centerline—from the ocean to her house the night before.

"Soon," Nate said. He finished wrapping her hands with cloth. He hadn't been able to find boxing gloves her size. She knocked the padded fists together. She had changed in the few weeks they'd been together. She moved like she wasn't thinking about every single move before she made it. It was a start. It wasn't enough.

"Put up your fists," he said. She raised them. Some of the

meek girl still there inside her. That was what Nate had to burn out of her if she was going to stay alive.

He fixed her shoulders, tucked in her elbows.

"The hardest thing about a fight is learning to get hit."

"You mean how not to get hit?"

"You're going to get hit," he said. "Life ain't a video game or a school test. There's no doing it perfect." Word for word the way Nick had said it to him. "You're going to get hit. When you do, your body thinks what's happening is that you're being murdered. And who knows, maybe you are. So your brain dumps a bunch of chemicals into your body, like rocket fuel."

"Fight or flight," Polly said. She was smarter than Nate had been at eleven, or fourteen when Nick had done this to him. Sometimes he thought maybe she was smarter than him now.

"Yeah, that's it," he said. "Either fight back or run, your body says. Only we aren't cavemen anymore. The world wants to teach you to not fight back, or even really run away. The world wants you to stand there and take it like a punk. So your brain dumps this rocket fuel into you and you don't do anything and all it does is make you burn right where you stand. You know what I mean?"

He listened to himself, to his tone. He couldn't hear the wavering he felt inside. He hoped she couldn't either. A thing like this was dangerous. You get it wrong the first time and you might not ever get it right. You might break something inside them.

"So when you're in a fight, a couple of different things happen. You get that crazy boost. That rocket fuel. It makes you wild, or it freezes you up. Either one is bad. You got to learn how to ride the rocket."

He put on his boxing gloves. He looked over to the bear, who she'd positioned to watch over their training. He nodded to the

bear like *what up?* He'd been catching himself doing shit like that
more often. The girl had a trick of making you forget the bear
wasn't alive.

Nate hunched down close as he could to her eye level. He lifted
his fists. She did the same. Polly mirrored him.

I'm sorry. I'm so sorry.

He didn't say it. He couldn't even show it on his face. He had
to keep his face calm, so she'd think this was okay.

He shot out a feather jab. It just touched her face. He watched
it set off earthquakes inside her. He felt them too. He saw her lock
her breath up inside her.

"Did I hurt you?" he asked her.

"No."

"Then don't act like it. Put up your fists."

He raised his fists. Polly raised hers. He flicked out the jab
again. A little harder this time. He felt the connection. Her eyes
went wide.

"That burn you feel inside you, that's the rocket fuel dump."
He cut an angle, popped another light jab. She swatted at it, wild.

"That's adrenaline. That's a gift from the deep down part of
your brain." He double-pumped the jab, first a high feint then a
low jab, tapping her stomach with the second. Animal panic in
her eyes. He pushed past the voices telling him to stop. He listened to the ghost of his brother.

Either you teach her how to take a punch or the world does.

"Adrenaline isn't bad," he said. "Just don't let it use you."

He bopped her on the nose. She slapped away his fist. Still
wild, but better.

"When the bullies came after you, when they hurt you, it
wasn't the hurt that you were scared of. It was what you wanted to
do, what you could do, that's what scared you."

He threw a left to her ear, harder than he meant it. Her breath clicked fast as a sewing machine.

"Get mad if you're mad," he said.

He threw a jab. She moved her head so it just grazed her cheek.

"That's right," he said. "You got to get free of it. Whatever it is that's stopping you from fighting. You got to climb out of the cage."

He one-twoed, let her catch them both on her forearms. He felt her breaking point coming. He didn't want to push her past it. He didn't want the lesson to be lost.

"The world wants you to sit on your hands and take what it gives you." He popped jabs at her, stinging her, stinging him.

"The world wants you scared of yourself. You have to let the blows come. You have to take them. You have to be ready. You can't go crazy. You can't freeze up. You got to take the punches. And then you got to punch back."

He pop-popped her on the eye. Saw rage bloom. He threw a light hook to her belly. He left his other hand low. He gifted her his face.

She swung. Her left fist fit in his eye socket. His teeth clipped in his skull. He sat back on his ass and caught her next swing. He watched her come back to the world.

"I'm sorry," she said. Eyes wide and deep.

"No," he said. "That's just how you do it. But don't let the mad take you."

She swayed on her feet.

"Breathe," he said.

She broke and ran for the bathroom. He listened to her empty her stomach. With her out of sight, he let himself cover his face with his gloved hands. He stood like that until he heard her flush the toilet. He knocked his gloves together loud to let her know he was coming. He walked into the bathroom. Polly sat facing the toilet. She wiped a wrapped hand against her mouth.

"We're doing it again tomorrow," he said. "And the day after that. Until you learn that a punch don't kill you."

She had tears in her eyes. But behind them, fire.

20

POLLY

—

HUNTINGTON BEACH

It was Polly's first kidnapping. From this side of it, anyhow.

They sat in the green monster outside the woman's house. Polly wore a baseball cap to cover her watermelon hair. When she ran into the liquor store for sodas, the old woman behind the counter had called her a little boy. She almost corrected the woman. But she let it ride. It didn't really matter, and she was undercover, after all.

Polly's muscles groaned under her skin. Aches were a constant thing now. Under the sore muscles her bones hummed like power lines. She felt them stretching at night. She'd need new clothes soon.

They drank sports drinks and bottled water. They peed at the taqueria down the block. They ate mulitas stuffed with steak. Polly ate as much as he did. She was always hungry these days.

They watched people come and go from the woman's house. Men with shaved heads, tattoos on their faces and necks. Women too. Her dad had explained the tattoos to her. How sometimes they had numbers, but it was like a code. Like how *88* stood for

HH stood for *Heil Hitler*. That the Woody Woodpecker tattoo they saw down a man's muscled bicep meant he was a part of Peckerwood Nation. The green-eyed woman, the one they watched, with her hair shaved everywhere but her bangs, Nate called that a "featherwood."

The green-eyed woman opened her door to all of them. From where Polly sat across the street, it looked like the woman said hello with her mouth but not with her eyes.

"It doesn't look like she likes them," Polly said. "Why do they come visit her?"

"She's a spider," Nate said.

"A what now?"

"A spider—she's at the center of a web," he said. "She's a connection between the inside and the outside. There's somebody she's close to who is in jail. A brother or a husband or something like that, somebody who is plugged in nice and tight with Aryan Steel. And she's passing him messages, and getting messages back. Probably running a bank account too."

"So she knows everything," Polly said.

"Yup."

"So she's going to tell us where their treasure is," Polly said. "And we're going to take it."

"Smart girl. But it's not easy like that. First she's got to tell us."

"She'll tell us," Polly said. "Or you'll make her tell us."

He scrunched his face, like she'd said something wrong. But it wasn't wrong, was it?

THEY DID IT the next day.

He put a blanket in the backseat so Polly could hide and listen. She climbed back there, the bear in her arms, as they rolled back onto the woman's block. She felt like a pirate climbing a rope ladder. She carried a ghost knife between her teeth.

"Yo ho ho," she said as she plopped into the backseat. Nate looked at her with a frown. But his eyes smiled.

Polly slid down to the floorboard. She pulled the blanket over herself so she could hide when the time came. They'd timed it just right. The mailman was just pulling away from the curb when they got there.

"Well all right," her dad said, watching the mailman go. "If we got her pattern right, she'll be out to fetch the mail in a minute. Be ready. It'll happen damn fast when it happens."

Maybe it was a minute or maybe it was ten before the woman came out. She wore a too-big T-shirt and cutoff jeans. She put on makeup just to get the mail. Wild red lipstick that Polly liked.

"Here we go," he said. Polly had that juiced-up feeling, like someone had just poked air holes in the lid of her jar.

"I'll be back," he said. "Something goes wrong, you run."

"I won't leave you," she said.

"Fuck that noise," he said. "You'll run."

Polly watched from the backseat as he walked to the woman's front door. He had a gun in his pocket. He reached the woman before she saw him coming. He put the gun against her. The woman looked like a person caught napping. Polly watched the woman's face get angry. Not scared. He wrenched the woman to the car. Polly slid back down and pulled the blanket over herself and the bear. Giddy now, giggling. Under the blanket the bear lifted a paw like *shush* when the car doors opened.

"What the hell is going on?" the woman asked. She didn't sound too scared. Polly liked that.

"I'm not going to hurt you," Nate said. "Not unless you make me."

"Fuck you." Polly liked her even more.

The engine started.

"All I want is some info."

A beat passed before the woman answered.

"You're not a cop."

"Didn't say I was."

"You got any idea of who you're fucking with?"

"You're plugged in with Aryan Steel," Nate said.

"Then you know you're fucking dead, right?"

"I'm already a goddamn zombie walking," he said.

Polly guessed the woman didn't know what the hell to make of that.

"They can only kill me once," he finally said. "So I can't be scared. Means I'm going to get what I came for. Why don't you make it easy?"

"Tell you what, cowboy. You let me go right now, go back to whatever fucking hole you climbed out of, and I won't say a word to Dick."

"Who's Dick?"

"Bullshit. You come after me, you sure as hell know who Dick is."

"All I know is you're a spider. You got a man inside. That who Dick is?"

Polly scrunched her face at the bear like *what are they talking about?*

"You know enough to know I'm not going to say a goddamn thing," the woman said. "You can't scare me any worse than I'm scared of them."

"We'll see," Nate said. The air under the blanket was getting hot. It was getting harder for Polly to feel like she was getting full breaths. She wondered if the woman would talk easy. She didn't want the woman to talk. She wanted to see what her dad would do if the woman wouldn't talk.

"I need places," he said. "Trap houses. Stashes. People moving product. Figure you ought to be able to draw me a map."

"Didn't you hear me when I said 'fuck you'?"

Polly heard the pistol click.

"You're not going to shoot me," the woman said. It sounded to Polly like maybe the woman was telling it to herself, hoping maybe she'd believe it if she heard it out loud.

"Playtime's over," he said. That was the sign for Polly to plug her ears. That something ugly and mean might happen. She didn't plug her ears. She raked her bottom lip with her teeth, harvesting strands of flesh.

"I'm not some goddamn junkie looking for a fix," he said. "They killed my ex-wife. They're fixing to kill my daughter and me. So you better—"

"You—you're Nate McClusky?" the woman said. "The one everyone is looking for?"

Polly pulled the blanket off her head before her front brain had even figured out what it meant. She sprang up behind the woman. The woman horror-movie screamed. The look on her face, the terror, made Polly feel like she could tear bricks in half with her hands. She got those monster hands into the woman's hair, close to her skull so her knuckles scraped the woman's scalp. She yanked the woman toward her. She opened her jaws like a girl raised by wolves. She leaned forward to take a bite of the woman's face.

"Polly, stop it," Nate said. He got his hand between Polly and the woman. Polly's teeth clicked hard as she bit air. Nate pushed her back into the seat. She came back to herself, a little.

"What the fuck," the woman said. Polly punched the back of the woman's seat.

"You're one of them," Polly said, her voice raspy and wet. "You're one of them who helped kill my mom."

"You're the little girl," the woman said. "Oh my god. I'm sorry. I'm so fucking sorry."

21

CHARLOTTE

—

HUNTINGTON BEACH

The way Charlotte saw it now, free will was a crock. She hadn't always thought so. She'd driven out to L.A. from Missouri at the age of twenty-two feeling wild and free, heading west like the old books said. The direction of freedom. She'd moved out to Huntington Beach, got a job as a waitress at one of those places where you wore low-cut tops and served chicken wings to guys who got handsier with each mug of beer. At least the tips were okay. She knew she was just treading water, but that beat drowning for sure.

She'd been at the bar long enough to learn the names of all thirty beers when one of the other waitresses said she was spending her day off visiting her brother up in Lompoc. She asked if Charlotte wanted to go with her. Charlotte was about to say no when she remembered her AC. It was the middle of July and her landlord was dragging ass on getting her window unit fixed. Charlotte didn't want to spend the day in a sweat lodge, so she'd told Vicki *sure, why not?*

Later on she'd think *what if the AC had waited one more week to go on the fritz? What if her landlord had had just one shred of human decency in him and had fixed it the day it broke?* That goddamn little condenser unit in a window AC had changed Charlotte's life forever. Who could contemplate a thing like that and then turn around and say it was free will that got her where she was?

She and Vicki took a road trip up to Lompoc. It wasn't until they got to the signs on the highway saying don't pick up hitchhikers, jail nearby, that Charlotte started to understand how real it was.

It got more real when they went through the metal detectors. A woman in a gray uniform and a dull gray face went through their purses. Then a guard pointed them down a hallway with only the words "no touching." Then she walked into the visiting room and everything changed.

Dick sat there in his prison blues, a man born for a broadsword and a horse, like the men on the covers of her brother's Dungeons & Dragons books, sitting in the visiting room like he owned the whole world. He looked at her and it was the same thing, like he owned her, or, closer to the truth, like he was thinking of taking her and the only question was *was she worth taking?* He didn't speak to her during the visit, just to Vicki, but at the end of the visit he turned over to give her a look and he asked her if they could trade addresses, write letters. She said, "Sure, why not?"

"A MILLION REASONS WHY NOT," her brother Alan said later. His voice was tinny, beamed up from the Ozarks to some satellite and back down to California. Three words in and Charlotte remembered why they didn't talk much, even times like now, times when she needed someone to talk to.

"Literally a million," he went on. "I could list them till Christ comes home. Let's start with what he did to get locked up in the first place."

"Manslaughter," she said. "It was a bar fight. Way he said it, he didn't start the fight, he just finished it."

"Hellfire," he said. "You already sound like one."

"One what?"

"One of those women. Those crazy jailhouse women making excuses for her locked-up man."

Didn't she know the type? Didn't she love those true-crime paperbacks, the kind with black covers and red type, and the center section of black-and-white photos? Those books were full of dumb women writing forever love letters to the Night Stalker or Charles Manson. And hadn't she read them and laughed and said just how hard up do you have to be?

"Tell me you won't write him," her brother said.

"Of course not."

And she hadn't. But she didn't forget him either, especially not at night when sleep wouldn't come and her blood rose like the Nile in her veins. But she put him at the back of her skull, where he seemed happy to stay. Until she got his first letter.

Later on when she had perspective, she understood it better. A man behind bars has nothing but time. They don't have the Internet or smartphones, beer buddies or side pieces. They don't have cable teevee binges, football parties, a career. When a man behind bars chose to focus on a woman, it was total focus. His first letter ran ten pages, the second one fifteen.

The men around her started to seem washed out and frail. Doughy men who'd never withstood anything meaner than a tattoo needle or a Jägermeister hangover. Dick felt like a man from another time. Hell, even the name. What man went by Dick anymore? The audacity of it. Soon she was dreaming of him. He'd take her, put his hands on her like he couldn't control himself, rip clothes from her, coax her with rough hands. The dreams came on her during the day, came on her like holy visions.

She threw away her promise to Alan. She wrote Dick her own letter. She told him about herself. Her job at the bar. Her asshole managers with Russian hands and Roman fingers. The girls who stole from the till. That she wanted a new apartment, something closer to the beach.

He wrote her back and told her to cut out the cocktail party bullshit. He didn't want to know about soap opera crap. He wanted to know her. He wanted a piece of her she'd never given to anyone else.

The letter pinned straight through her—a butterfly to a board.

So she wrote him, eleven pages front and back written between hand cramps on a long Sunday. She wrote him about the worst thing she knew about herself. About 9/11. How she had felt bad the way everyone had felt bad, but that there was another thing mixed up with the sad. The thrill. How exciting it was to watch the towers fall, the clouds of dust enveloping the world, the geysers of flame jetting out of buildings, the bodies falling on camera, the thuds. She knew it was real and she knew it was a tragedy but it made her feel alive all the same. She'd been a junior at Kickapoo High School in Springfield, Missouri, and up until then, her life had been a gray blur, and when those towers came tumbling down it felt like maybe life wasn't something that just happened in movies. She felt she'd been told a secret that day, something beyond what they teach you in school or that you learn from your parents. Something so terrible and bright inside her that she had to put a blanket on it or it would overwhelm everything. Her whole life—hell, the lives of everyone she'd ever met—

was built around being safe, but first of all, safe was a lie, and anyhow there were better things in life than being safe. Maybe it was better to live in a world where towers fell.

Telling him about that was her way of letting him know she was his. He got it. He claimed her for real the next visiting day. He put a hand on her leg. It was as rough as she'd dreamt. He let her taste danger by proxy. He told her about his business. That he was a lieutenant in a gang called Aryan Steel. That he had soldiers beneath him. Generals above. That he fought for them, and killed. She drove back down the 101 to L.A. in a dream while the sun sank hissing into the ocean to her right.

A few visits after that, he told her he needed her help. That she was going to open a bank account. People were going to give her money. That she was going to buy a cell phone that couldn't be traced. That people were going to call her on it.

She drove home telling herself to cut him off. To go back to her life. She looked down the road of that life, how it was straight and narrow. That was the phrase they used, like it was a good thing. Straight and narrow.

The next visiting day, she found herself there waiting for him with a bankbook in her hands.

He brought her into his world. She didn't like his world. She didn't like the friends, the women dumb and vicious, the men with cruel eyes and meth stains on their hearts. By the time she thought to look back at the shore she'd swum away from, it had receded from view. She was stuck in the middle of the ocean.

She'd passed hundreds of messages. Sometimes they came in coded letters. Sometimes they came in phone calls with a lot of "the guy with big eyes" and "the place by the other place" type language.

The only one that ever stuck to her was the death warrant

against Nate, Avis, and Polly. It had come to her straight from
Dick's mouth. He'd made her repeat it to him. The words were like
bad milk in her mouth, but she'd said them all the same. She'd
said them to Dick so he'd know she'd learned them, then she went
home and she said the words to the cruel-eyed men and vicious
women. She'd heard about the woman on the news a week or so
later. It was like she'd flicked a domino and a week later a tower
fell.

And now, sitting next to the man, the little girl staring at her,
she had to face that at least that one time, she hadn't been made
to do a thing. She'd made her choice. She'd passed the message
along. This was on her.

SHE LOOKED AT THE GUN. She looked at the girl. Her anger ebbed away.
The fear too.

"Tell me what you want to know," she said.

"Everything," the man said. The girl didn't say a thing. She
had a teddy bear in her arms and murder in her eyes.

22

POLLY

—

HUNTINGTON BEACH

While her dad questioned Charlotte, Polly took notes with a pencil pebbled with tooth marks. She'd found the pencil at the bottom of her school bag, and the notebook too. She tore out the pages filled with division problems and facts about South America. She dropped them crumpled to the floor. She wrote ARYAN STEEL at the top of the page. She drew a line underneath it. She numbered the different places.

Charlotte talked to Polly's dad, sneaking peeks at Polly, looking away, touching the claw marks on her face where Polly had gone after her. Polly liked the way Charlotte looked at her, like Polly was a monster wearing little girl skin.

Some of the words Charlotte used, Polly understood. Some she didn't. She wrote them down anyway. She figured her dad knew or he'd ask. She wrote down things that seemed important. Like this:

CHOP SHOP—mechanic on Alverado s. of McArthur park.
Close to chicken place. Peckerwood Nation.

She mouthed words to the bear as she wrote, not because she had to but because they were fun to say. *Peckerwood chop shop peckerwood chop shop.*

She wrote about a trap house by the Hollywood In-N-Out. An Odin's Bastards biker bar on the PCH. A Peckerwood Nation safe house in Venice Beach. A white power metal bar in Encino. The main stash house down in Sun Valley between the scrap yard and the garbage dump. This last one was the one that her dad asked the most about.

"What kind of stash house?" her dad asked.

"Crank," Charlotte said, and Polly wrote it down even though she didn't know what it meant. "The main stash for the Nazi Dope Boys."

Polly wrote quick as she could.

"That might be the one," her dad said.

"You want to hurt them, that's what I'd do," Charlotte said.

"You been there?" he asked.

"Once," Charlotte said.

"You can draw it? The inside, I mean."

Charlotte nodded like *I guess so.* Polly handed her the notebook. She pulled herself up by the back of Charlotte's seat to watch her draw. Polly kind of liked the fake-flower smell of her. She peeked over at her dad. He kept his eyes on Charlotte. Something in his eyes when he looked at the woman made Polly feel off balance.

"Is that all?" she asked to break the heavy silence.

"Who runs the operation?" he asked.

"They call him A-Rod."

"That's a baseball player," Polly said.

"Yeah. He's a hitter," her dad said. "It's another word for killer."

Charlotte nodded like *that's right*.

"So he's trouble," he said.

"No shit," Charlotte shifted in her seat to look back at Polly. "Sorry about that."

"It's okay, I can hear curse words," Polly said. "He says them all the goddamn time."

"Polly . . ."

The bear shook with silent laughter. He slapped his leg with his paw. Polly caught Charlotte clocking the bear, a look on her face like *nutso alert*. She fought the urge to put the bear away. What did she care if this woman thought she was nutso?

"You're really going to do it?" Charlotte asked. "You're going to rob that place? These guys are killers—"

"Think we don't know that?" he asked. Charlotte turned away fast like the words had slapped her.

"I guess you do," she said.

"I get the feeling they know that we're coming, I get the idea you said a word to anyone about this, I come back to see you," Nate said. "And you won't see me coming."

"I say a word about this to anyone," Charlotte said, "and dude, the line to get me will be long."

THEY LET HER GO in front of her house. Polly watched her walk back to the door. How Charlotte looked back over her shoulder. How he looked back at her with that same hungry face of his that made Polly grab the bear tighter in her arms.

"When you go rob them, you're taking me, right?"

"It's not pretend, Polly. It's men with guns who won't stop themselves from hurting a little girl."

"There's men with guns anyway. If you're doing it I want to do it. I want to help."

"It's dangerous," he said.

"You said it was dangerous everywhere for us. So we should be together. I want to help."

He didn't talk for a while. He shot sideways eyes at her, breathed out a long slow breath.

"Then you help."

"Okay," Polly said. "But you have to tell me what to do. I never robbed anything before."

23

SCUBBY

—

SUN VALLEY

Up until the moment the girl with the cherry soda hair and crazy blue eyes came to the door, Scubby considered himself a lucky man. At least for a suckmouth son of a bitch such as himself. Someplace in this wide world maybe there was a better job than official crank taster for the L.A. Nazi Dope Boys, but whatever that job was, Scubby didn't want it. The way Scubby saw it, he was sitting prettier than the pope in Rome. Sure, that pontiff motherfucker had silk drawers and a billion people under his thumb, but he had to wear a silly hat and go to church every day. Scubby? He was doing what he loved.

Check it out: Three lines of crystal lined up on the table. See how each one was a little different shade of white? This one paper white, this one snow, this one bone. Scubby had an eye for the little things. That was his job.

A-Rod stood next to Scubby rubbing his row of blue thunderbolt tattoos. He liked to let his hands linger over the bolts when he thought Scubby was getting out of line. Just his cute little way of reminding Scubby that one of them was a killer and one of them wasn't. Scubby knew A-Rod didn't want him around. He knew that while A-Rod was king shit of the Nazi Dope Boys, he was just another peon in the Aryan Steel army. He knew A-Rod didn't think he needed a crank taster but had been overruled by the boys inside. He knew A-Rod didn't know all the angles. Scubby knew the angles.

When the crank was cranking at the base of his spine, Scubby read everything. He read every article in the newspaper and then he read the ads, and the backs of cereal boxes and shampoo bottles, and the ingredients on the back of the kitty litter. He'd read about the War on Drugs, and methamphetamine, and how there was a three-way arms race afoot in the Southern California drug trade. The cops, the cartels, and the peckerwoods. Used to be back in the day, meth was a pretty easy cook. There were a couple different recipes, regional differences mostly. Then the government started cracking down. The feds outlawed ephedrine. Two things happened because of that. One was that down in Mexico where ephedrine was an easy find, they started cooking more meth. The other thing that happened was that the peckerwoods started finding other ways to cook. Back in the day there'd been smurfing. That's where you'd go from gas station to gas station, grocery store to grocery store, and you'd buy every scrap of decongestant or antihistamine they had.

Then the cops would change the laws again, and the cartels would shift their recipe, and the peckerwoods would shift theirs, like some sort of arms race. The Nazi Dope Boys moved major crank through Southern California. They brewed it out in the desert, outside Hangtree, where the law smiled on dirty white-boys. He'd heard about slabs of concrete left in the desert by an army base, a town of RVs and Quonset huts, a desert meth plant to rival those of Mexico. They called it Slabtown. It was all under the thumb of some crazy sheriff named Houser who took a big bite to keep the Mexis out and keep the labs cooking. Houser was a dream come true for the whiteboys. Not even the cartels would consider hitting a cop, not on this side of the border.

The meth came in from Slabtown through Odin's Bastards. The bikers moved it into L.A., to A-Rod and the Nazi Dope Boys. They brought it to the Depot, the house in Sun Valley where Scubby at this moment was letting these thoughts run wild. From here the Nazi Dope Boys packed the dope and moved it up and down Southern California. To Fontucky, San Bernardino, up north to Ventura, all the way up to Bakersfield.

Odin's Bastards, the Dope Boys, everyone in the game, they all kicked up to Aryan Steel. A-Rod here carried two passports. He was a big-time shot caller for the Nazi Dope Boys, but he was a mere soldier for Aryan Steel. So if the Steel told him to employ a taster to figure out which cook out in Slabtown had the blue-ribbon recipe, that's what he would do. But that didn't mean he had to like it.

Scubby took down the paper-white line. Jagged broken glass up his nostril. The pain was a good sign. The First Law of Meth: for each burn, there is an opposite and equal rush.

"Legit," he said as firecrackers *pop-pop-popped* in his brain.

The snow-white line was barbed wire pulled down his throat. Tears sheeted his eyes. He sang a snatch of "You Dropped a Bomb on Me." A-Rod's face killed the chorus half-sung.

Scubby shook his head, made cartoon noises, picked up the bill to try the last line—

Knock knock knock.

A-Rod pulled up his shirt, showing a flat black pistol. Scubby gripped the table like the tornado was about to hit. Ghost cops flickered in the corners of his eyes. A-Rod waved the pistol like *go on, get the door.* Scubby spelled out *fuck no* with his face. A-Rod stopped waving the gun. He pointed it at Scubby. Looking down the barrel of a gun, you don't see the tip of the bullet. You just see darkness, like a preview of eternity. Scubby went to the door. He pressed his eye to the peephole.

A one-eyed teddy bear looked back at him.

Methamphetamine psychosis. Too much crank piled on adrenaline had turned his brain into a fried candy bar.

He went back to the peephole. Got a different angle. Looked down as far as he could. Saw the bear was stuffed in a backpack, its head sticking out the top. Saw the top of the head of the person wearing the backpack. This girl with Kurt Cobain eyes and hair like cherry soda.

"Who is it?"

"It's a girl," Scubby said.

"The hell you mean a girl?"

"Like a teenage girl."

"That shit has turned your brain to snot," A-Rod said. He pushed Scubby aside. He peeped the hole. He whistled. He said, "I'll be damned." He undid the four locks. He swung the door open, the gun behind his back.

"Hello there, little lady," A-Rod said. The way he said it made Scubby think of a honey-dipped knife. It must have been that way for the girl too, the way her face changed.

"My dog ran away," the girl said in a singsong. A-Rod tossed his pistol out of sight.

"Oh no," A-Rod said to the girl. "Your dog. He's your buddy, I bet. Maybe I can help you." Sirens went *ahooga* in Scubby's brain

as A-Rod undid the chain and swung the door open for the little
girl.

The world went action movie.

The girl stepped aside and out of nowhere came this badass.
Jailhouse swole, jailhouse tats, same crazy blue eyes as the girl. He
had a sawed-off in his hands.

A-Rod moved toward the badass. The badass swung the
sawed-off so A-Rod and the shotgun butt smacked like a head-
on on the highway. A-Rod's nose burst. An arc of blood splashed
itself across the coffee table, crisscrossing the last line of meth.

The little girl pulled the bear out of the backpack. It fucking
waved at Scubby. Methamphetamine psychosis still seemed viable
as an explanation.

A-Rod lay on the floor, his face a red mess. The badass moved to
Scubby. Scubby saw himself reflected in the man's eyes—no muscle
tone, nostrils as red as a prison punk's ass from all the rails he'd
gakked down, the spreading patch of piss in his jeans—and knew
the words NO THREAT might as well be tattooed across his head.

"What's your name?" the man asked.

"Scubby."

"Where's the stash, Scubby?"

"Don't you tell them," A-Rod said through a mouth full of
red stew.

"Coat closet," Scubby said, nodding to it. A-Rod spit ugly
words and broken teeth.

The girl handed Scubby something. He looked at his hands
and saw the girl had given him a roll of duct tape.

"We got to tie you up," the girl said. That singsong to her voice
again. Scubby placed it now. She'd memorized her lines. "It'll go
better if you help us."

Scubby taped A-Rod's hands behind his back. When he was done he looked up to see the girl holding the bear like a puppet, the bear nodding at him. Behind her, the badass had the grocery bags with the dope in them.

"This all of it?" he asked Scubby.

"Yeah."

The man placed the sawed-off's barrels to his head. Scubby could feel every metal bump where the shotgun's barrels had been sawed-off—whoever'd done the job hadn't done it well, and it still had splinters. Scubby wondered, if his brains wound up on the wall behind him, would the little pieces keep thinking for a minute, all alone, the piece of meat that held the words to "Shook Ones" just singing to itself while it cooled on the wall?

"Are. You. Sure?" the man asked.

"Uh-huh. Ought to be about ten bricks. That's the whole load."

The man studied Scubby like he was doing a pro/con list on killing him. If there was a drop of piss left in him, Scubby would have let it out right then. But there wasn't, so the muscles down there just did a painful squeeze instead.

"Don't hurt him," the little girl said. "He doesn't have any blue lightning. This one does." She nodded at A-Rod, at the blue lightning bolts on his arm. The way she said *this one* splashed Scubby like icewater.

"I know who you are," A-Rod said, rocking himself up to his knees. "You're the zombie. And this little cunt—"

The badass shut A-Rod's mouth with his boot. He went backward. With no hands to catch him, his skull hit the floor full force.

The girl moved the bear's paws to cover his eyes. The bear shook his head like *oh no this is terrible*. The girl was a hell of a puppeteer. But from the light in her eyes Scubby wasn't sure the girl agreed with the bear. She didn't think it was terrible at all.

The badass tapped blood off his shoe against the coffee table leg like a man knocking off snow.

"You tell them it was Nate McClusky," he told Scubby. "You tell them to pass it down the line. I'm not going to stop till they lift the greenlight on my girl. Now who am I?"

"Nate McClusky," Scubby said.

"And Polly too," the girl said. And the man looked over at her and he smiled and the girl smiled and Scubby felt for sure that none of this was real and he was staring at a white wall someplace where they only served you food you could eat with a spoon.

"And Polly too," the man said. "You tell them."

And then they were gone and Scubby sat back on the couch, still not sure what was real and what wasn't.

"Cut me loose," A-Rod said. Scubby thought about it. The way he saw it A-Rod was going to have a lot of frustration to work through when he got untied. And there was only one stress ball in the building.

"Naw, man. Sorry," he said. "But I think I'm just going to moonwalk the fuck out of here."

"You fucking think about this."

"I will," Scubby said. "From a great distance."

"When I find you—"

"Yeah, I know. I sure hope you don't."

The final line of crank from the test batches on the table was freckled with red dots where the blood from A-Rod's nose had splattered it. *Fuck it,* Scubby thought. *Who knows how long it will be before I find a new hookup?* He gakked the line, A-Rod's blood and all. Inside him volcanoes erupted. He tasted battery acid and sewage. He tasted A-Rod's blood. Maybe A-Rod passed on a little bit of his spirit, cannibal warrior style.

"For what it's worth," Scubby said on his way out the door, "that one's the winner-winner chicken dinner."

He hit the air a free man. Sun Valley smelled great for the first time ever. Free air smelled great, even when it was filthy.

24

POLLY

—

SUN VALLEY / NORTH HOLLYWOOD

The girl was a bandit now, and she knew a bandit's pleasure. She could tell her dad felt it too. He drove fast. He took lefts and rights that seemed random, but Polly knew it was all planned out. Polly powered down her window and stuck her head into the wind like a dog. She tasted the night. Her body was a single thing, from the tips of her toes to the ends of her hair dancing on her skull.

They passed an SUV with a woman behind the wheel and kids in the back, their noses pressed against the glass so Polly could see the boogers. The bear mooned them. Polly laughed. Her dad laughed. The light changed. He gunned it. Polly shrieked wild noises of joy. She tumbled back in her seat.

"Come on back," he said. "Come on back to earth."

She came back slow. She wondered what Madison Cartwright was doing just then. How small she seemed now, how pinched and ratlike her face was, that same face that had seemed impossibly pretty to Polly before.

"I never thought it would be so fun," she said.

"It isn't always," he said. "Now put on your seat belt. Last thing we need right now is to get pulled over just for having a kid with no seat belt."

"I'm hungry," she said as she buckled up. "Can we have pancakes?"

The bear rubbed his stomach like *yum*.

"The bear votes yes," she said.

"Funny how he likes all the stuff you like."

"He likes you," Polly said. The bear leaned over and kissed him on the cheek. "See?"

Polly pulled open the paper bag. Plastic bricks of white powder. She held it gingerly away from her, like it might explode.

"This is meth?"

"It's bad news," he said.

The bear walked down her lap to peer into the bag. He stuck his head into the bag. He came out shaking like he was electrified.

"Oh no," Polly said, laughing so she worried she would pee. She threw the bear up in the air like jumping. He bounced off the green monster's ceiling and crashed to the floor. Her dad laughed and laughed.

"Drugs are bad," she told the bear. She rubbed stomach muscles sore from laughing.

"For real, what will we do with it?" she asked.

"Dump it," he said. "All we want is for them not to have it. We don't need it."

"Do you think it will work?"

"What do you mean?"

"Will they quit?"

She wasn't sure what the answer would be, or what she hoped it would be. She wanted to be safe, to sleep through the night without waking up at the slightest noise. But when it was done, she didn't know what their lives would be. He had told her one night about a place called Perdido. A town in Mexico where everybody was somebody who'd run away from the world. A beach town that wasn't on any map. An outlaw resort, a place for them. Because she was an outlaw now. Would she be the only girl?

"No," he said. "They won't quit just yet. We're going to have to hurt them a lot worse than that."

She didn't know if she was happy or sad. But she knew she had to feel that feeling again, that bandit joy.

The white powder was bagged up in little plastic bags, the kind kids at school used for carrot sticks. When they got back to the apartment, after diner pancakes, Polly opened the first package, dumped it in the toilet. She thought the toilet would maybe bubble like witch's brew, but the powder mostly just disappeared. She grabbed a second bag.

"Dump it slow," Nate said from the door. "It eats pipes. We don't want to have to call a plumber."

"It eats pipes?"

"Told you it was bad news. I'm going out," he said.

"Where?"

"Just out," he said. "Want me to bring you something back?"

"Candy," she said.

"You already had pancakes," he said.

"So?"

"You're in training," he said back.

"Just a little piece," she said. "One piece of candy."

"All right then."

She flushed the toilet, grabbed the second bag, and dumped it in.

"Put a towel over your face or something," he said as he left.

She pulled her T-shirt over her mouth. She kept dumping. When she was done she moved over to the sink, her shirt still over her face so she looked like a bandit.

She was a bandit.

She pulled the shirt down. She looked at herself in the mirror. The bright red hair, the color she'd picked for herself, the hair almost boy-short. The way the man with the blue lightning on his arm had looked at her when he'd opened the door came back to her, ruined her good mood. She struggled to find the right words for what had been in that gaze. He had looked at her like she wasn't a person exactly, more like she was a roast chicken on the plate and he was trying to figure out which piece to eat first.

She touched the glass. She was glad that her dad had hurt the man who had looked at her like that, and she felt bad for feeling good. It seemed when she was a kid she only ever felt one thing at once. She could be happy or sad but she'd only be that one thing. Now she never felt only one thing. It was like walking wearing two different-sized shoes. Nothing was ever level or smooth.

"Maybe I should dye my hair back normal," she told the bear. The bear shook his head *no*. He reached forward and stroked her hair. He gave her a thumbless thumbs-up.

"I like it too," she said. "Fuck that guy."

25

NATE

HUNTINGTON BEACH

He acted like he didn't know where he was driving. Like he was just out clearing his head. Like he didn't know he was heading west.

He knocked on the door. She opened it a crack. He could tell from the way she was standing she had her foot wedged behind the door. Already showing more smarts than that suckmouth had at the stash house.

"I told you everything I know," she said.

"That's not why I'm here."

"Why are you here then?"

"We hit the stash house today."

"I don't want to know."

"They're going to be asking questions," Nate said. "They'll get around to asking you soon enough."

"Take your daughter and get the hell out of California."

"There's no place safe for us," he said. "That's why we're fighting."

Headlights lit them up as a car rolled down the street. Nate touched the gun in his hoodie pocket. She saw the move. And Nate saw how it scared her but that she liked it too.

"You got to leave," she said. "You're crazy to be here."

"I know," he said. "Can I come back?"

"Why?"

"You know why."

He could see in her face that she did. That it wasn't his imagination. She had wild eyes. Same as he did these days. He understood then how they'd got to her. How he'd got to her too. Then something in her—something smart, Nate had to admit—won out. She shook her head *no*.

"Just find yourself somebody who doesn't know who you are," she said.

"You already know my secret," Nate says. "And I know yours."

"The hell you do."

"You've been living in a cage you built so slow you didn't even notice when the door locked behind you. And you maybe even haven't let yourself admit you want out."

"Please go," she said.

He stepped back from the door to say *okay*. He turned away. He knew he had to leave it up to her.

"I'll meet you someplace," she said behind him. "Someplace nobody knows me."

26

POLLY

—

NORTH HOLLYWOOD / ENCINO / KOREATOWN / GLENDALE

These next days were the best of them all, so good and wild that later on Polly could only remember them in choppy flashes all out of order.

Food tasted different again, like a layer of dead skin had been scraped off her tongue. They kept eating Mexican food, lots of it. Soft tortillas with pork-fat warmth. Crisp pork, sour pickled onions. Sauces bursting red or green, fire on her tongue, fire down her throat. Her dad couldn't handle the heat. It made him sweat and hiccup. But she loved it. "You get that from your mom," he said, and it hurt to hear that but it helped too.

She was growing; she could feel herself growing, her skin stretching, a dull ache in her nipples at night.

They settled into a routine. She hadn't realized how much she craved one. They woke, they did exercises. Push-ups, jumping jacks. Prison-yard exercises, he told her. He figured out how much to push her. She learned to like being pushed. To like misery.

He taught her how to box. How to shoot out the jab like a cannon shot, how to bring it right back so she wouldn't be open. How to raise the hands to keep herself safe.

He taught her how to wrestle. How leverage turned into strength. She got the physics of it. Levers and fulcrums became chokes and wristlocks. Sometimes she dreamed of wrestling faceless people. Sometimes winning, sometimes losing.

He taught her how to fight dirty. Thumbs in the eyes, fish hooks. She blushed when he taught her to kick a man in the crotch. How weird evolution was, she thought, to put that stuff there like a shut-off switch between a man's legs.

In the afternoons she read books they found in secondhand stores. She practiced chokes with the bear. Afterward they danced. They found out all three of them loved big loud hip-hop. The bear did the twist, the swim. He shook, he skanked. She made him dance song after song.

There was a thing they never said to each other, a thing that ought to be said, dad to daughter and daughter to dad, but later on she'd know that even though they never said it, it was true, that she felt it with everything she had and that he had too, and surely that was good enough.

At night, they hunted.

Polly began to live for that time from the moment you started the job to the moment it ended. It was like stepping out of a rocket ship to take a space walk.

They took down a white power club in the Valley. TONITE STEELTOE H8 on the sign above the door. Polly kept watch from the driver's seat, her hand hovering over the horn to give the two-honk signal if something went wrong. Music bled out the windows of the building, low bass notes, drums like machine gun fire. She bobbed her head to the beat.

Kids with shaved heads so fresh their scalps were ghost white, their swastika tattoos drawn on in markers, ran as her dad moved into the club with the sawed-off. He took the gate money while the Odin's Bastards bouncer foamed at the mouth and swore vengeance. Later that night they bought steaks at the grocery store with white power money. They grilled them at midnight, gobbled them down rare. Pink juices on her chin, down her throat.

THERE WAS A CHOP SHOP TOO, maybe before the club, maybe after. They broke in at two in the morning, Polly manic from robbery rush and no sleep. She giggled while he boosted her through a broken window. He passed her the gas cans and the Sterno bomb he'd built that afternoon. She doused the room. Gas fumes stung her eyes. She heard a *bok-bok-bok* and she wondered if gas fumes had driven her nutso. But no, there it was again. Even though her heart did crazy things she followed the clucking. She opened an office door. She found a rooster in a cage, black with a bright white Mohawk of feathers. She passed the cage over to her dad through the broken window before she lit the wick to burn the place down.

"It's a fighting cock," he told her as they drove away from the garage, the bird squawking in the backseat.

"I couldn't let it burn," she said. The bear put a friendly paw up to the cage. The rooster pecked it. It said *fuck you* in chicken.

They let it go in MacArthur Park. They shooed it into the night. Her dad tried to chase it. It spread its wings. He kept his distance.

"Are you chicken?" Polly asked. The bear knee-slapped.

The night turned red and loud from fire truck sirens on the street below them. The rooster flapped into the dark. Now they were both laughing. Her dad put a hand on Polly's shoulder and squeezed. She rested her hand on his as they watched the big fire engines roll past them.

"Did we do that?" she asked. She knew the answer. She just wanted to hear him say it.

"We did that," he said. She leaned against him. Breathed him in. The flashing lights of the fire engines strobed against their faces.

TINY TIM was an Aryan Steel tax collector, and he was the biggest person Polly had ever seen. Her dad explained it to her. How all the whiteboy criminals in the state owed taxes to Aryan Steel. Ten percent. They called it *the dime*. Tiny Tim's job was to collect the dime.

Tiny Tim had to duck his head to avoid hitting it at the top of doorways. Sometimes he forgot. He finger-fished his nose and ate his catches every moment he didn't think he was being watched. Polly and her dad, rolling behind him in the green monster, had to hold their laughter in like kids in church. Polly pressed her face against his shoulder to block out the hilarious sight of it.

They followed Tiny Tim all day. He carried a backpack with him. It got heavier every stop. They followed him to a house in Little Armenia.

"We'll do it here," her dad said. "You know what to do?"

She nodded like *yeah* and asked, "What's here?"

"It's a place men go," he said.

"There's women in there," she said.

"Yeah."

"Ladies of the night," Polly said. He laughed. "Shut up," Polly said. "That's what they're called."

"Where'd you get that?" he asked.

"I read," she said. "Don't laugh at me."

"Ladies of the night," he said. "Here he comes."

Polly's skin got all tingly, the way it did before their missions. She'd learned that the energy that flooded her body was fuel. Before, she'd been a rocket ship stuck in its docking even as its engines roared, burning itself. Now she flew.

She looked up to see Tiny Tim *thwack* his head on the door-frame as he walked out the door. He rubbed his stubbly scalp as Polly slipped out of the car. She stood to face him as he reached the sidewalk. She tasted sweetness on the air and said, "Hey mister." Tiny Tim turned to her. Her dad came up behind him. He kicked Tiny Tim behind his knee, and the knee crackled like burning wood as the big man dropped. His scream was higher pitched than she would have thought. Both his hands flew to his crushed knee. Polly grabbed the backpack. The two of them ran to the car. They burned rubber.

She opened the backpack. It was stuffed with money almost to the rim.

"Holy shit," Polly said.

Polly counted money. Thousands of dollars. They flapped in the wind like palm fronds.

"We're rich," she said.

"Not yet," her dad said. "But we will be."

"What's that mean?"

"The next job," he said. "I think it's the last one. The one that will make them quit."

That should have made her feel free. Instead, she got that trapped-rat feeling she hadn't felt in weeks. Like Venus was ascendant.

"What is it?" she asked.

"The Steel's bank," he said. "That big dude was just one of the tax collectors they've got. There's one for every part of L.A. that has whiteboy business. And when they've made their collections, they take them to this old warehouse in Chinatown. It's where they hold the money before it's shipped off to be laundered. We hit that, we can buy our way out of the greenlight."

"How'd you learn about the bank?" Polly asked. "Charlotte didn't tell us about that place."

"She told me," he said. All sorts of wrong notes in the music of his voice. The music of Venus ascendant.

The car walls closing in on Polly. Her clothes tightening like a snake.

"When?" she asked.

"Last night," he said. "I've been going to see her."

Polly threw a double-handful of cash out the window.

"SHE'S ONE OF THEM," Polly said to the bear once they were back in the house.

"Talk to me, not him," her dad said.

"She's one of them," she said. But what she meant was *you lied to me.*

"She's not like that," her dad said. "She's a kid who got confused. She's helping us."

She'd never seen him look so weak before. Not even when he'd been shot. She turned away from him, not wanting to see his dumb face. She tried to shove the lid back on the pot inside her. Bad thoughts bubbled over anyway. *Ruined,* they chanted. *We're ruined.*

SHE SPENT HOURS training herself, sweating, punching pillows, rolling on the floor. Anything that kept her brain in the moment.

She was choking out a pillow when he opened the door from the bathroom and called to her. She kept choking the pillow, going through the checklist in her head. Move hand here, squeeze here.

"Polly," he said again. "Come here. Stay pissed if you want, but you got to see this."

She walked into the bathroom. Nate had stripped off his jeans. He hiked up his boxer shorts to show her the place where he'd been shot. It had been getting better, almost healed up all the way. But now it was purple again. And at the center of it something hard and gray bloomed.

"Is it infected?" she asked. The word *hospital hospital hospital* looped in her head.

"No," he said. "Touch that gray part."

She moved her hand to it, slow. Her fingers brushed hard metal.

"It's the bullet," he said.

"The bullet?"

"I've heard about this," he said. "My body's rejecting it. It'll keep crawling out my body until one day there'll be enough of it for me to grab and just yank it like a big ol' splinter."

And she could see by his eyes that he liked it. He thought it was cool. Polly didn't. She didn't believe in magic, not at all. But it felt like an omen. Like the gods' way of saying nothing stays buried forever.

WHALE SHIP CANNIBALS

THE HIGH DESERT

LUIS

HANGTREE

It was the sort of hunger that turned whale ship sailors into cannibals. It had Luis fucked up bad. It racked his muscles. It chilled the Cali desert air until he shivered. It turned the faucet on in his nose. Call it junk hunger, aka dope sickness. It pushed everything else to the sides of his mind. The handcuffs biting into his wrists. The fact that he was in the backseat of a cop car headed to jail.

The hunger came with a load of irony: Luis's stomach was stuffed with the very thing he hungered for. His gut swelled under his T-shirt thanks to fifty capsules packed with the heroin he craved.

Water, water everywhere.

Luis had gagged the capsules down one at a time in the back room of a Tecate bar. A couple of *chuntaro* cartel badasses in polyester shirts and Jesus Malverde cowboy boots mimed it out for him: take a condom stuffed with capsules, dip it in oil, swallow it, sip water, repeat. They left him with some works—a spike, a spoon, a lighter for cooking, a cotton ball to filter the cooked junk—and a good shot's worth of Mexican brown. It would have been enough to keep Luis on even keel until he was back in the arms of Frog-town Rifa, back to the carnales who would fix him up good. It would have been enough if everything hadn't gone to hell.

He'd been nailed thirty minutes past the border, just outside a shitkick Cali desert town called Hangtree. Hadn't even been a speed trap. The cop car rolled out from a side street and pulled in behind him like it'd been waiting for him special. The cops ordered him out of the car without even putting on a show of running his driver's license. They cuffed him and put him in the back of the squad car, leaving the car abandoned at the side of the road, the door still open.

Not an arrest. A vanishing.

The one with the badge that read SHERIFF HOUSER had mirror shades for eyes, a gray bristle mustache, hands that could tear an apple in half. He gripped the wheel with scarred knuckles. The man made no wasted movements. He drove through red lights and stop signs like they were invisible.

The cop sitting shotgun looked like something escaped from the bowels of the earth, fat and pink and nearly hairless. Houser called him Jimmy. When Jimmy took off his sunglasses, his tiny squint eyes told Luis that the man had been called pig way before he ever pinned a badge to his chest. Jimmy snuck looks back at Luis and flashed a clown's smile. The smile made Luis's balls want to crawl up in his belly. His belly told his balls, no room at the inn. No room for anything but dope-filled condoms and the hunger.

The cruiser rolled through Hangtree, what town there was

to roll through. The citizens stiffened as the cop car passed by—every soul in Hangtree looked to be riding dirty. Missing teeth. Tweaker eyes. The air that came through the car vents carried the rotten egg smell of meth brewing.

The cop station loomed ahead. Luis pictured kicking cold turkey in a jail cell. His one hope: somebody—La Eme, those crazy Nazi bastards in Aryan Steel, hell, even the *mayates* in the Black Guerrilla Family—had a source in the lockup.

The cruiser rolled past the cop station without slowing down. Maybe they were taking Luis straight to a hospital, get a doctor to stick a hose up his ass to wash the capsules right out of his intestines. But Luis's junkie instincts said this whole deal was wrong—wrong far beyond getting pinched with class-A felony weight in his stomach.

They drove up into the high desert. The road twisted. They passed through some sort of encampment. Old concrete slabs set into the earth. Campers and homemade shacks set up on the slabs. The shacks and campers had chimneys. Spray-paint pentagrams. Green bottle glass shattered and set into concrete spelling out SLABTOWN. A dead tree, its branches heavy with old shoes. The unmistakable smell of meth cooking overpowered everything. They passed a man naked but for a butcher's apron, a surgical mask pushed down under his chin so he could smoke. He nodded at Houser like *morning, boss*. Houser touched the brim of his hat like *howdy*.

They came out the other side of the village. Houser turned the car onto a dirt road up into the hills. The bad vibes turned seismic.

"Where you taking me, man?" Luis asked.

Jimmy giggled. He wiped sweat off his head with a crusty handkerchief. The car kicked up dirt clouds as it climbed. Gravel churned under the tires. The road leveled off. Ahead of them Luis saw a fence, chain link and razor wire, around a windowless cinder-block building with a rusted metal door. Luis's stomach dumped acid—*what-the-fuck* piled on top of the dope sickness.

"He's not looking too good, boss."

Luis looked up to see Jimmy eyefucking him.

"Reckon he's got himself a thirst," Houser said.

"Never know how a man lets himself get that way," Jimmy said.

A pit dog—face scars, torn-off ears, death in its eyes—rounded the corner like something out of a detox nightmare. It came to the chain-link and stood man-height, huge paws poking through the chain-link.

"Don't you?" Houser asked. "A fellow does something makes him feel good, so he does it again. Same way we trained the dog."

"What the hell's the dog got to do with it?"

Houser shut off the car, pointed at the monster behind the fence.

"Some folks dress their dogs in little outfits, talk to them, treat them like human beings. And some people point and laugh. They say dogs aren't people. And they're right. Dogs aren't people."

The old cop climbed out of the car. He walked through the desert heat like it was made for him. Lizards sunning themselves on the path fled from around his feet.

"Dogs ain't people, no shit," Jimmy said as he pulled Luis from the backseat.

The dog eyed Luis hungrily. Grinding rocks burbled deep in its chest. Houser unlocked the fence. He made a signal with his hand. The pit dog sat. He chained the pit dog to the shaded side of the building.

"No," Houser said. "Don't you see? Dogs aren't people. People are dogs. They come when you snap. They run wild when no one's looking. Feel shame when they're done. They lick the hands of the strong and snap at the weak. They destroy because they are bored. They chew up the things they love. They need the pack. They hump what they can, eat and drink what they can even when they'll sick it up later. They give love to those who show them love, even if the giver is no good and rotten and mean. Dogs aren't people. People are dogs."

"That include me?" Jimmy asked.

"Indeed it does."

Houser unlocked the door of the building.

"It include you, boss?"

"No. I'm not people." And Houser gave Luis a smile that proved the point. *Oh shit oh shit,* Luis screamed inside his skull.

Inside the shed was dark, sweatbox hot. The heat punched him heavyweight hard. He dropped to his knees on a cracked concrete floor. The piggy one laughed. Luis pictured a dozen deaths for the bastard. He wished on them. But they did not come true.

"Cut his hands loose," Houser said to Jimmy. Jimmy yanked up Luis's hands behind his back until his shoulder blades ached, sawed him loose from the plastic cuffs with a utility knife. Houser took Luis's hands in his own, dwarfing them.

"You know who you're fucking with?" Luis asked them. "Come on, you got to know. I'm with Frogtown Rifa. We kick straight up to La Eme. You don't steal from the Mexican Mafia 'less you stupid."

Houser took off his mirror shades, his eyes underneath somehow colder.

"They know where I'm at," Houser said. "They're welcome to come see me any time."

There it was. Luis knew what Houser knew. No one, not even

La Eme, hell, not even the Sinaloa cartel, would order a hit on a cop this side of the border. Mexican cop lives were cheap, cheap as junkies like Luis. But a U.S. cop was untouchable. Only way to take out a dirty cop was another cop arresting them, and when did that ever happen? This ice-cold son of a bitch was bulletproof.

Only good part of that: maybe it meant Luis could walk away. Maybe Houser was so balls-out sure of himself that he could let Luis live. Why not? Who could Luis tell? What trouble could he bring? Then Luis remembered that smile and the hope left him.

"You're on the take, man." Luis wished his voice wouldn't tremble like that. "We rolled past a dozen labs on the way up here, and you don't give a shit. So there's got to be a deal we can work out."

"You tryin' to bribe a cop, son?"

"You a cop, then take me to fuckin' jail, man."

"Yeah," Houser said. "I'm a cop, all right. I protect those who pay me against those who don't. There's never been a cop in history where that wasn't the gig. And it turns out that the folks who pay me the best ain't too big on the competition. Especially brown folk like yourself."

He took Luis's head in his massive hands.

"All they care about is that you Mexi boys learn this part of the desert ain't for you."

Jimmy had something in his hand. A plastic sandwich bag with something like twisted twigs at the bottom.

"Can we feed him?" Jimmy asked. His eyes all excited pleading. "MK-Ultra his ass."

"We got business," Houser said. "We don't got all day."

"These magic mushrooms I took off one of them Joshua Tree hippies," Jimmy said. "Gonna learn how to mind-control people. Like the CIA MK-Ultra."

"It's what's in his belly now that we're after."

"But boss—"

Houser cut Jimmy off with a look.

"Now we know what you got stowed away in you, boy, and we're going to have it. So you're going to do what you need to do to produce it for us right now, or we're going to have to deal with it the other way."

Luis got the picture. He pulled away from Houser. One hand on the floor to steady himself, two fingers of the other hand down his throat. His throat jerked around his fingers. His stomach rebelled, emptied on the floor. Bile and slop. No capsules. He tried again. He coughed thick ropes and sour acid. His nose ran. Tears welled. He heaved. Dry. He tried again. Dry.

"Reckon they're too far down the road to turn back," Houser said. "Like the rest of us. Jimmy, get the lights, huh?"

Green-glow fluorescents stuttered to life overhead. Luis saw a table set in the center of the room, manacles at both ends. He saw a second table with knives, scalpels, a bone saw curved like a bladed smile. He saw rubber gloves and plastic bags. He saw a hose ran from a sink to the table.

A homemade surgery theater.

"Jesus," he said. He rose swinging. Houser caught his wrists, forced him down to the ground. Jimmy got an arm around Luis's throat. He fought back on autopilot, pointless. He burned out fast. He flopped back in Jimmy's arms.

"Sorry, we just don't got the time for your load to come out the other end," Houser said. "Going to have to head it off at the pass."

Jimmy giggled at this as he moved his arm off Luis's throat to make room for his knife. The last thing Luis knew was the pain and the hunger leaving his body, just one second of peace before the nothing kicked in . . .

27

NATE

—

CHINATOWN

Matchstick weather. That's what Nick had called it back in the day. When the wind shifted and hot dry air came in from the desert, sucking the water up out of everything, making it seem that the world begged to burn. It put Nate on edge.

They parked a half-block down the street from the bank. This was just observation. Nate wanted to do this one right. He'd gotten sloppy, let Polly's wild enthusiasm spur on dumb choices. He had to do this one cold as hell. This would be enough cash to buy their freedom. Maybe even enough to get them to Perdido. By then Polly would have defrosted. She'd have to.

A street corner fruit vendor chopped mangoes and pineapples nearby. Nate had bought Polly a soda, a peace offering. She hadn't accepted it. She ran the sweating can against her sweating forehead, but she didn't open it. The cup holder held the .38, covered with a newspaper.

"You can turn on music if you want," he said, then wished he hadn't. He had to stop giving her everything.

"No," she said. She breathed out against her window, her mouth an O. She fog-painted a circle on the window. She made eye dots with her thumb. She drew a straight line for the mouth.

Jesus, this kid.

This part of Chinatown wasn't Chinese. It was artists and low-budget filmmakers taking advantage of the low rent. And in among them, looking like just another warehouse, was the bank, just the way Charlotte had described it.

Charlotte. Just the thought of her peeled a layer of civilization off him, coughed up memories that were all sensation and sound and smell.

"What's going on?" Polly's words brought Nate back to the now.

A beat-up pickup truck rolled to a stop in front of the house. The man behind the wheel had sunglasses and a splint over his busted nose. Three blue bolts on his arm. Under all the stuff the face looked familiar. Polly placed it before he did.

"It's A-Rod," Polly said. She slumped in her seat.

"Put on that ball cap," Nate said. "Now."

She reached for the Dodgers cap from the backseat and pulled it on. She checked herself in the sideview mirror. She stuffed stray red locks up under the hat.

"What's he doing there?" she asked.

The men took down the door of the truck. From where they were parked, Nate could see into the truck bed. He saw a tarp. Plastic sheeting. Shovels. Big bags of something—Nate bet it was quicklime. A portable body-disposal kit.

"He's taking somebody on a last ride," he said.

The alley door of the bank opened. Two skinheads walked a kid out onto the street. The kid had *oh shit* eyes. He had dreadlocks. Nate knew him right away.

"It's the other one," Polly said. "Scubby. The one who helped us. What are they going to do to him?"

Nate let Polly work it out on her own. She was a smart girl. She figured it out.

"He's going to kill him."

"He should have run," Nate said. "We gave him his chance."

"We have to save him," Polly said, stress fractures in her voice.

"No we don't," Nate said.

"No no no," she said. "You can stop them. He's going to die because of us. We made him help us and now he's going to die for it. It's not okay. You know it's not okay."

His hands ached. He was strangling the steering wheel.

"Daddy, you can't let him die."

"To keep you safe I can. I will."

"I don't want to be safe," she said. "Not like this."

"Close your eyes. I'll tell you when to open."

"I don't want to—"

"Close your goddamn eyes, girl."

She covered them with her hands. Nate watched it all.

Nate couldn't read lips. You didn't have to to get what Scubby was saying. He begged with his eyes. Nate promised he'd add Scubby to the list with Avis and Tom. Add his face to the ones he saw in the dark. The ones who had died because Nate kept on living. He promised the kid some kind of justice. The ghost of his brother laughed in his head. Nick always could sniff out bullshit.

He heard the shotgun door click open. He turned to see Polly already on the street. She ran toward the alley.

Goddamn that girl.

Nate knocked aside the newspaper, reached for the pistol hidden under it. His hand touched sweating aluminum. The pistol was in Polly's hand. She'd left her unopened soda in its place.

28

POLLY

—

CHINATOWN

You have to save him.

It wasn't her brain telling her. It wasn't her mom's voice. It wasn't anybody but Polly talking now. She wouldn't let anybody else die.

Her body exploded in a full-on sweat. The day was locked-car hot. A car shrieked to a halt as she pounded across the street. She didn't even look at it. Somebody swore in some language she didn't know.

You have to save him.

The gun felt impossibly heavy in her hand as she moved into the alley. But she carried it anyway. She came into the alley on a deep breath. A-Rod had his hands on the kid's shoulders. The two men who had led the kid out of the bank stood close to the truck.

"Leave him alone," Polly said. But her voice came out a rasp of no words. She said it again, still raspy but louder. The men looked at her. Their faces were all different flavors of *what the hell?* She pointed the pistol at A-Rod. It only shook a little.

"Please let him go," she said, and knew she'd done it all wrong. You don't say please with a gun. She blinked. The world jittered. The evening lights all of a sudden too bright.

"The fuck are you doing here?" A-Rod said, like the gun was invisible. He smiled that weird wolfish smile. She hated him. She heard her dad say *never touch the trigger 'less you're going to shoot.* She felt her finger curl on the trigger. Her brain cataloged everything. Every sound. Car horns honked. Someplace a helicopter whirred. Motors growled. Music flowed from a dozen cars. Every smell. Rotting vegetables. Car oil. Old pee. All of their faces. A-Rod's hand lingering behind his back. The kid with his soft brown eyes so full of red-web little veins, so full of pleading. One of the men from the bank was smeared all over with tattoos. The other one was cleaner, with a couple of wet tattoos and scared eyes.

Muscles flittered and jerked all over Polly.

"Grab her," A-Rod said. "She's worth a franchise."

The one with all the tattoos moved on her. Like she didn't even have the gun. Like she was nothing but a little loser girl with slumped shoulders.

"Come on now," A-Rod said. "She ain't going to shoot."

Polly pulled the trigger. The pistol jumped in her hands. She fired it dry in seconds.

29

NATE

—

CHINATOWN / SILVERLAKE / NORTH HOLLYWOOD

Nate sprinted across the street. He had the soda can in his fist. Gunshots *bang-bang-bang-bang-bang-banged* out of the alley. Crazy screams on the street. He reached the mouth of the alley sure he'd see his little girl dead on the ground. Knowing if it was so he'd die here too, one way or another.

But Polly stood three steps into the mouth of the alley, her back to them. The .38 in her hand smoked. A-Rod stood facing Nate. Scubby and the fresh skin pressed themselves against one of the brick walls behind them.

The inked one had a hand slapped against his neck. Blood leaked out around his palm where one of Polly's bullets had clipped him. He moved toward Polly. He kicked her to the ground. He raised his own big-ass pistol to Polly's head.

"Hey!" Nate yelled. He threw the soda can fastball hard. It cracked into the inked man's face. The can sprang a leak and whooshed down the alley. The inked one's hands covered his mangled nose. He sank onto his butt. The wound on his neck where Polly had grazed him yawned. The big-ass pistol skittered on the pavement. Nate moved in front of Polly, picked up the big-ass pistol. Hoped the damn thing wasn't for show.

A-Rod and the young one fell back in the alley. A-Rod got behind a dumpster. The young one pointed his gun at Nate. His hand moved like he tried to pull the trigger but the gun didn't shoot. He didn't know enough to see the safety was on. The kid ran. The kid reached the other end of the alley and kept on going.

Scubby broke past A-Rod. He hustled past Nate and Polly out into the street. A-Rod rose up from behind the dumpster, some kind of hunting rifle from the truck bed in his hands. Finger-snaps around Nate's head told him death had missed him by a hand's length. Nate raised the big-ass pistol. The pistol had an extendo clip. It banged as fast as Nate's finger could move. Gun-shot echoes everywhere. Tires squealing in the street. *Oh my god* screams from passersby.

Nate stood in front of Polly like he could protect her, like he could stop bullets. He walked backward, pressing into her. He kept shooting. He pinned A-Rod behind the dumpster.

They cleared the mouth of the alley. He and Polly ran. Skin-heads stood in the doorway of the warehouse. They stared dumb at him. He waved the pistol at them.

Weird quiet in the city now. Their feet *slap-slap-slapping* pavement seemed so loud. Sirens rose in the distance. Nate looked to-ward the car. Scubby stood waiting for them at the door of the green monster.

"Get the fuck out of here," Nate said. He raised the pistol. The slide locked back showed that he'd emptied it.

"They'll kill me," Scubby said. "Just get me out of here, please, man."

It wasn't worth the fight. Nate pushed Polly across the driver's seat. Scubby threw himself into the back. He smelled like fresh piss laid over dried piss. Nate jabbed the key into the ignition. It roared to life hurricane loud. His foot was already stomping the gas. The ghost of his brother cut through the sounds and insanity.

Breathe, little brother.

Nate did. He didn't peel out. He pulled slow into the street. He craned his neck looking for cops. Listened for a chopper. He took a right. A left. Polly kept begging. Apologizing. Crying. He looked over, saw tears streaking through blood on her face.

Blood on her face.

"Where's that blood from?" Inside he pled to whatever wasn't cold and dead in the universe.

Please take me instead. Me for her.

"What—"

"Where's the blood from, Polly?"

He touched her face. Showed her the blood on his fingers. Her eyes went wide.

"I'm okay," she said.

"Feel," he said. "Feel around. You don't always know you've been shot."

She felt all over her body as Nate hit the on-ramp to the 101. The gods smiled just this much: traffic rolled on the freeway. They entered its flow smoothly.

"I'm okay," she said again. This time it sounded like she meant it. Nate felt muscles unclench. Felt the sweat popping all over him start to do its job as the day drank it. He took Polly's hand in his.

She had the bear locked in a headlock hug. She wiped tear-snot on her sleeve.

He knew right then it was over. *Me for her,* he thought. A warm thought that made him cold. *Me for her.*

"That shit was bananas," Scubby said from the back. Nate had forgotten he was there.

"Pick a place," Nate told him. "And make it close."

AT SCUBBY'S DIRECTION, Nate pulled off the 101 at Silver Lake Boulevard. The underpass was a tent city. The people living there dirty faced and unfed. Refugees of a war only they knew about.

"You're good here?" Nate asked.

"Good as I'll ever be," Scubby said. "Goddamn. They caught me slipping, no shit."

"I see you again, I kill you," Nate said.

"There's a club for that," Scubby said. "I think they meet on Tuesdays." He nodded to Polly. "Later, wild child. Thanks for missing."

He ducked through a tear in the chain-link and walked into the tent city. The bear waved goodbye.

They parked in front of the apartment building. Nate let the engine tick over.

"I'm sorry for what I did," she said.

"You wanting to save that dumbass, it was a good thing," Nate said. "But you could have died. When I heard that gun go off . . ."

"You thought I was dead. You didn't think it was me shooting?"

"I didn't know what to think."

"I missed."

"You were wild," he said. "A little handgun like that, you can't be wild."

"Next time I'll be calm," Polly said.

He was going to tell her then that there wouldn't be a next time. But before he could, a shadow broke itself away from the side of the building. It moved toward the green monster. Just enough time for Nate to realize all the guns in the car were empty, to know it could happen this fast.

30

CHARLOTTE

—

HUNTINGTON BEACH / KOREATOWN / NORTH HOLLYWOOD

Charlotte had been in full relaxation mode when they came for her. She wore an old Electric Wizard T-shirt and some boxers. Her blown-glass magic-mushroom-shaped bowl stuffed with some indica. Diet soda and rum. A bag of chips. A plan to get baked and watch sitcoms until she drifted off to sludgy sleep. She had just torched the bowl. She played dragon, made *rar-rar* noises when she exhaled smoke. She touched the red flesh on her wrist where Nate had held her. At the thought of him her cells all rubbed together, a low and beautiful drone all through her. Trysts in backseats, in cheap motels, all flavored with the thrill of being a double agent. Nate had a lot of the things in him that had drawn her to Dick. The big difference was, being with Nate didn't make her hate herself. It scared her in ways both bad and good, but she didn't hate herself.

The doorbell chimed soft, but it shocked her like a klaxon. Just stoner paranoia, she figured. She padded to the front door.

The double-agent voice inside her said *keep the chain on*. She kept the chain on. She opened the door. A featherwood named Kim stood on her porch popping gum. Beauty-mark piercings on her cheeks. Pancake makeup over rubble skin.

"Hey," Kim said.

"Hey," Charlotte said. Stoner paranoia goosed her. Kim had never visited her. They'd talked at parties, at the beach, those weird soirees with beer and hot dogs and white power talk. Charlotte struggled to recall anything about Kim other than she hated her dad and she drank Midori like a teenager.

"There's a thing at the beach," Kim said.

They know.

Charlotte looked over Kim's shoulder to the car parked out front. Smoke and rockabilly drifted from the car windows. Blurry man shapes inside. She couldn't make them out to know if she knew them or not. But she could feel their eyes on her.

"I don't know . . ."

"Come on," Kim said. "We'll swing by the liquor store, then hit the beach."

They know.

"I'm sort of in for the night," Charlotte said. She wondered what windows in her house were open. How fast she could get them all shut. If something like that would even stop them.

"You sure?" Kim popped her gum. Her eyes were flat like a lizard's.

"Yeah," Charlotte said.

Pop.

Pop.

Pop.

"Okay," Kim said with a smile that said *we know*. "Maybe later."

"Bet," Charlotte said. She shut the door. She leaned against it waiting for the kick to come. She ran to the kitchen, pulled a butcher's knife from its stand. She ran down the hall past the living room where her ice cream melted. She came in, grabbed her cell phone, and ran back to the hallway. She slammed the bathroom door shut behind her, feeling how flimsy and hollow it was, how easily a kick would bring it down. She climbed into the bathtub. She dialed the nine and the one and the one and held her thumb hovering over the call button. The knife clenched in the other hand. Hours passed like that, every creak or thud in the night rolling through her like a missile impact. Near four in the morning, when the weed and adrenaline had moved mostly through her, she formed a plan. She left the bathroom, knife and phone at the ready. She packed a bag. She went out into the night. Dashed to her car. Waited for them to come for her. But they never came.

She drove into L.A. Everything in the city seemed so much closer together when the traffic was gone. She found an all-night diner in Koreatown. She ate beef soup with drunk twenty-something Korean kids in club clothes. She drove to the Valley, found a side street, and slept in her car. When she got to the address Nate had given her during one of their nights together, they were gone. She waited for them. It was just past nightfall when she saw his car pull up. She went to the car window and found Nate pointing a pistol at her. The girl sat shotgun. She had blood on her face.

31

POLLY

—

NORTH HOLLYWOOD

Air is a soup. It's how planes can swim through the sky. With Charlotte in the house now the soup of the air had thickened almost to jelly.

Polly and her dad still trained in the morning. But it was different now. Charlotte watched them. Polly could feel her eyes. Polly's punches missed more and her chokes weren't as tight.

Ruined.

He made a bed for himself on the couch so Charlotte could take his room. A dumb lie told for nobody. Polly could feel unsaid things in every word between the two of them. A language she almost understood, but didn't quite.

Charlotte kept her distance from Polly. She smiled those big dumb smiles adults used on kids when they didn't know how to act around them. Her voice too loud like little ears couldn't hear as good.

At night there were no more hunts. They ate takeout dinners.

They had the money from Tiny Tim's backpack, enough to last them months easy.

"But it's not about money," Polly said on the second hunt-less night, as Charlotte spent the forever she always spent in the shower. "It's about making them quit, you said."

"It's time to change plans," he said.

"Because of her."

"No," he said. "'Cause of Chinatown."

"I won't do it again. I promised already. I said I was sorry."

He looked at her that old way, that *I'm grown-up and you're not* way that made her want to scream.

"It's time to change tactics," he said. "Way back at the beginning, you said if Crazy Craig was the president of Aryan Steel and he was the one who wanted us dead, we should just make him not be president anymore. Remember?"

"I guess."

"Well, you were right and I was wrong. We can't keep trying to bleed them out with little cuts. I can't have you in the line of fire anymore."

"I want—"

"I can't have it," he said with eyes like *do not push it.*

"So what then?" Polly asked. "Time to go to Perdido?"

"I don't even know if Perdido is real," he said. "Could be just a dream."

"We can find out," she said.

"There's someplace I'm going," he said. "Someplace you can't go."

"You promised," Polly said. "You promised we'd stick to-gether."

"Where I'm going is just a bar," her dad said. "No kids allowed. That's all."

"So I won't go inside. I'll hide under a blanket."

"Fine," he said.

"Because you promised. You promised we were a team."

For a long time there wasn't anything between them but the shower's white noise and thick, thick air.

"Yeah," he said. "I promised."

And she knew he meant it but she also knew there was something else, some other deeper lie beneath it.

32

NATE

WALNUT PARK / FROGTOWN

Nate walked to the door of the Dew Drop thinking about how gunslingers die. Billy the Kid, Wild Bill Hickok, Jesse James. All three of those bad boys died without knowing it was coming. Wild Bill took a bullet in the head while playing cards. Jesse James took one with his face to the wall, straightening a picture. Billy the Kid died in the dark, asking *who is it?* to the man who murdered him. That's how gunslingers died. Real life didn't give you a showdown. Real life put a bullet in the back of your head.

At places like the Dew Drop.

Me for her.

He walked in the door.

The Dew Drop was a cowboy bar. Not dumb hats and country music. Cowboys as in operators. Heavies. Nick had called them life bars, as in *for people in the life.* Usually they were owned by ex-cons, guys who had come out the other side. Guys who weren't in the life themselves anymore, but who knew guys and could make connections.

The Dew Drop had barred windows. Inside was dim, lit only by a couple of bulbs and a couple of neon signs. The pool table had a path worn down the middle by a thousand breaking cue balls. It smelled of old smoke that twenty years of a smoking ban could never scrub out.

The Dew Drop belonged to La Eme. The guy behind the bar was a classic cowboy, Mexi edition. Jail tats faded gray on his arms. He had canyons on his face and the eyes of a man who had been hunted once. You never lost the eyes, Nate guessed. Once you were hunted, you could never rest again.

Nate sympathized. He knew the war had changed him forever. He was so goddamn tired. He slept in snatches, small noises in the night waking him like cold water on his face. A gun under his pillow. He slept so little his dreams had started leaking into his waking life. Just in small ways—a creature moving in the corner of his eyes, but when he turned to see it there was nothing there, shit like that. Sometimes he heard noises, people calling his name. He didn't think he was crazy, just tired. But he couldn't be sure. How would he know?

He sat at the bar. The old hardcase walked over.

"Do you for?"

"Beer to start. Whatever's cheap."

The hardcase pulled a bottle from ice. Nate paid for it, pushed across a twenty.

"Keep that," he said.

"*Gracias,*" the old man said, pocketing the twenty. "You just come home?"

"Susanville."

The hardcase's eyes danced over Nate.

"Did a bit there once myself," the hardcase said. "Where were you?"

"B-71."

"Hot as hell when you were there?"

"Only when it wasn't freezing."

The hardcase nodded like *that's right*. It felt to Nate like the exchange of passwords.

"You got a name?" the old hardcase asked.

Nate dug into his pocket, pushed a thousand dollars across the bar like *that's my name*.

"I need to talk to some carnales. I need someone close to the root. Someone who can get a ruling from La Eme."

The hardcase left the cash on the table.

"Going to need more info than that."

"I want to put somebody in the hat," Nate said. "Somebody on the inside. A big name. That's all I'm going to say for now."

The hardcase eyechecked Nate. Nate let him look. You didn't have to look mean. You just thought about where you'd been. Your eyes would do the rest.

The bartender took the money. Nate's eyes had passed the test.

"Tomorrow," he said. "Round this time. I'll scare somebody up for you."

POLLY AND THE BEAR poked their heads out from under the blanket in the back as Nate started the car.

"Did you find them?"

"Maybe," he said. "Got to come back tomorrow."

"You think it will work?"

"Yeah," he lied.

They drove for a while, Nate turning it all over in his head.

Polly played drums on the dash. She had the bear practice punches. Nate looked at her and felt his heart crawl up his throat.

Me for her.

He could have laughed at how fucked up life was. That soon as you found something to live for, you found something to die for too. But he guessed in the end it was a good trade.

HE CHECKED BACK in every day for three days. The hardcase just said wait. Nate waited. He trained with Polly. He watched Charlotte try to break through to the girl. Wondered how on earth she could be good enough for what he needed from her.

On the third night, they sat around the house post-dinner. Dodgers on the teevee. Polly on the floor, as far as she could be from Charlotte and still be in the room. She folded the bear's legs into the lotus position.

"What's he doing?" Charlotte asked. Polly mean-mugged her. Charlotte held the gaze.

"Come on, what's he doing?"

"He's meditating," Polly said, that old *are-you-going-to-laugh-at-me* tone in her voice. Nate almost interrupted, worried that Charlotte would dig the trench between her and Polly even deeper.

"That's cool," Charlotte said. "He's a good bear, huh?"

Polly placed the bear's paws facing up on his lap. The yogi pose complete.

"He's a ninja," Polly said.

The bear put a paw on his snout like *shhh.*

"No shit," Charlotte said. "Like an assassin?"

"He's a good ninja."

"What's that mean?"

"He goes on missions. Like at night when we're asleep. Like maybe he hears a kid crying, so he takes a bow and arrow, and shoots some ice cream into the kid's mouth. That's a good ninja."

Charlotte laughed.

"I never knew that," Nate said.

"You never asked," Polly said. She and Charlotte shared a look and it felt to Nate like something twisted into place, something locked.

Maybe it would be enough.

The fourth day, the bartender put his beer down in front of him, gave a nod, and Nate knew right away the nod wasn't meant for him. It was a signal. Nate heard steps behind him. He wondered if he'd feel the bullet if that's what was coming.

A guy took the seat next to him. His wifebeater showed off the black-hand tattoo on his bicep. It marked him as La Eme for life. His eyes did the same.

"You been looking for us?" A voice dragged through the ashes of a thousand cigarettes.

"Yeah. Need work done."

"I hear you, dog. Only you look the type to put in the work yourself, you know what I'm saying?"

"My name is Nate McClusky." He saw how the man's face didn't change. He already knew who Nate was. "I need to put a name in the hat. Somebody on the inside. Somebody big."

"Pay for your beer," the man said. "We're taking a ride, me and you."

"My daughter's in the car," Nate said.

The man smiled.

"That's the legend. My name's Chato. Get your daughter, man. She's safe on my mama's name. We're going to Frogtown. There's a council waiting for you."

Nate took the man's measure. Nate didn't know he had any choice but to trust him now. He hoped Chato loved his mother.

THEY DROVE A TWO-CAR CARAVAN through the city. Chato drove fast. Nate ran red lights to keep up. It jangled his nerves. Made his cop paranoia redline. Polly sat shotgun and watched the world pass. She was growing like wildfire now. Like she moved through time faster than the rest of the world.

They parked by the big concrete canyon called the L.A. River. The smog-blurred buildings of downtown rose in the distance. Polly let the bear dangle from her hand as they walked. They walked into an apartment building courtyard, Nate and Polly two steps behind the man. A double handful of apartments ringed the courtyard, but no sounds of life emerged. No cooking smells, no music. No burble of children playing. This wasn't an apartment complex. This was a fortress. They passed two baby gangsters not much older than Polly. They tried out their mad dogs on Nate. Nate let it slide. The bear in Polly's hands didn't. The bear waved at them. They got confused. They lost their mad dogs. Nate laughed. Gunfighter-death thoughts cut the laugh off early.

The apartment complex had a community center attached. Outside it, two young carnales. Their mad dogs were a significant improvement over the last pair. Chato opened the door to the community center. It stank of weed smoke and spilled beer, sweat and gunpowder. Nate knew if the room was empty, he was dead. He walked through the door anyway.

The room was full of full-tilt-boogie La Eme soldiers. The carnales were veterans. They were old school. They were dappled with shank scars and bullet wounds. They wore ink letters on their knuckles so their fists spelled out words. LOVE/HATE. FIST/

FUCK. IRON/WILL. They kept their jailhouse swole on. Seeing all these killers made Nate relax. They were going to listen to him. It meant he was going to live. For another five minutes, anyway.

The man in the center of them all radiated pure king power. El Hombre himself. Boxer Rios. Nate knew the stories. Boxer was the biggest La Eme soldier on this side of a prison wall. Aztec gods of war crawled over him. Warriors held bloody hearts aloft. The ink on his scarred knuckles spelled out STAY/DOWN. The ink looked old. He was the father of the style. Boxer studied Nate. His mad dog terrifying, nothing but empty rooms behind his eyes.

"So you're the guy been giving the Steel fits, huh?" Boxer asked. His voice throat-cut raspy. "You and this little *chica* here. You a little outlaw, *chica*?"

"Goddamn right," Polly said. The bear nodded like *uh-huh.* The carnales laughed.

"Little badass. Hear you're real bad for whiteboy business."

"Give it to him," Nate said. Polly walked toward Boxer, fishing a brick of cash out of her backpack. Boxer eyeball-counted it as Polly moved back to Nate's side.

"About five grand. What you trying to buy with it?"

"My life. My daughter's life."

"That ain't mine to give," Boxer said. "The greenlight on you, that's straight whiteboy business."

"I get it," Nate said. "I want you to touch somebody I can't touch."

Boxer nodded at one of the carnales. They vanished the cash.

"So you want somebody put in the hat, huh? Maybe you tell me who that is."

"Crazy Craig Hollington."

Boxer smiled like *whiteboy fucking loco.*

"You say it like it's no thing," he said.

"I can't touch him. You can. You want more than the five large, tell me what you want."

He held back the last bargaining chip. The one he knew they'd take. The one he didn't want to pay. But he would if he had to.

"I think," Boxer said, "when it comes to taking out the president of Aryan Steel, I think it's a seller's market."

"Word on the street is you and the Steel are in a cold war," Nate said. "They're cutting into your business a little more than you'd like. Maybe the next president will be more friendly to y'all."

"You think I need some *gabacho* stickup artist telling me La Eme business? Don't try to play above your weight, dog."

"Name the price for Crazy Craig. Any price. If I can pay it, I will."

"The cash, dog, we'll call that payment enough that I let you walk out of here, don't turn you over to the Steel myself. That's what the cash bought you. But you and the little badass here, you ain't got nothing I need."

Here it was. The last chip.

"I got one thing," Nate said.

"What's that?"

Nate walked toward Boxer. Polly started to follow. Nate gave her a *hold-back* hand signal. She stayed. Nate got close to Boxer. He whispered his offer to Boxer.

"Respect," Boxer said. "You got balls. But I'm going to pass. It's too big, dog. Too big."

Nate felt the world give way. This was the only shot he had. He couldn't let it pass.

"Think about—" Nate said. Boxer cut him off.

"I told you, you don't get to tell me how to play my game. Now you and your little girl, you leave—"

"I like your tattoos," Polly said, and Nate almost jumped.

Boxer looked at her like *huh?* She walked to his throne, Nate too surprised to think of stopping her until it was too late. She pointed at Boxer's chest, over his heart. "'*Gracias Madre*' means 'Thanks Mom,' right?"

"That's right, little badass."

Under the words on Boxer's chest, a cartoon drawing of a woman's face. A tear in her eye. Polly reached forward and touched the drawing.

"Crazy Craig killed my mom," Polly said. Tears wet down her voice. "She never did anything to anybody and she's dead. She was my mom."

Carnales traded *holy shit* looks. They traded *little badass* looks. Boxer reached for her with his STAY/DOWN hands. He took Polly by the chin. He mussed her watermelon hair. He nodded.

"Maybe there's something, little badass. Maybe there's something. But it's too big for just me. I got to make a call. Got to check with the inside. But maybe there's something."

Polly turned around to Nate. The face she made, only for him, only lasted a split second. *Ha ha,* her face said. *Fooled them,* it said.

He'd never been so frightened of her.

33

PARK

—

LOMPOC

Park hated prisons.

Prisons smelled like human shit and armpits. They sounded like the inside of a maniac's head. The light was always too bright or too dark.

Park hated prison leads.

Prison leads always worked an angle. Prison leads were only given for reasons. A love of truth and justice was never one of the reasons. That didn't mean they were bullshit. That was the problem. If they were all bullshit, he could have ignored them.

Park's life had bled to grayness in the two months since he'd talked to Polly McClusky on the phone. His leads had dribbled out. He'd put together what he could. The murder of Ground Chuck Hollington leading to the Aryan Steel greenlight. He'd even found the punk kid in Susanville, the one who'd tipped Nate off the night before his planned murder. Crazy Craig had made one mistake. He'd wanted to wait to hit Nate and his family the day of his release. Some sort of maniac irony. This punk kid, a Steel hanger-on, had passed a warning to Nate. "He didn't fuck with me," the only reason the kid could give.

Park had been able to put together where Nate had been. But where he was now, that was still a straight mystery. The media had lost interest the second week. A starlet found floating facedown in a Hollywood Hills home had grabbed the spotlight. The media was a living organism, and it ate beautiful dead things. Polly got forgotten. Park got other cases. He couldn't get a buzz going. Park wondered how he could get it back.

Then, two days ago, Miller had passed along a tip. An Aryan Steel heavy named Dick Carlyle in Lompoc wanted to talk. Noteworthy, as Dick Carlyle was a big fish who had never snitched before. Ghosts floated in Park's skull. He made the trip up the coast telling himself to ignore the buzz. To not get hooked again.

Dick Carlyle sat in Lompoc's interrogation box like he owned it. His legs spread wide, giving his balls plenty of air. He had eyes that made you reach back and touch your wallet. He had a smile like *fuck you*.

"You help me, I help you," Park said as he sat. Keep it simple. "First thing I need to know is what you want from me."

"A favor to be named later," Dick said. There were layers in his voice, warning Park that Dick here was a master cellblock manipulator. He'd hide his angle inside an angle.

"You can have an ask," Park said. "But you don't get to own me."

"I'm just trying to be a good citizen here," Dick said, bullshit so transparent it counted as honesty.

Park showed him Nate's photo.

"You know this guy?"

"You think he killed his old woman, huh?"

"No," Park said. "I think you guys did."

Dick did a good job of covering his surprise, but not quite good enough.

"But you're looking for him."

"Kidnapping is still a crime," Park said.

"Just want to make sure this tip ain't a waste of time is all," Dick said. This was the angle, Park realized. The first one, anyway.

"You want him on the inside," Park said. "So you can touch him."

"So?"

"So maybe I'm no Aryan Steel errand boy."

"What you going to do, stop looking?"

Park stood.

"Me Chinee, me drink Coke," Dick said. He pulled his eyes slanted. He busted up laughing.

Park had never hurt a man before. Not just to hurt him. He didn't know where to start. The thinking about it made the moment pass. Dick saw him, like he was naked. Dick dropped a major eyefuck on him.

"Get one of the screws in here if you can't get it up," he said with his *fuck you* smile. "They don't mind slapping us around."

Park gripped the table. Knuckles popped. He kept the pot from boiling over.

"Tell me what you have to tell me," he said.

"Word is he's in L.A.," Dick said. "Word is he's taking down Steel businesses. He's taken down serious weight. A lot of crank. A lot of taxes. He's nigger rich now but he's still going. He says he won't quit till the Man Himself knocks off the greenlight."

"Sounds like bullshit."

"Check out the Chinatown shootout. Your boy Nate's been running and gunning. He's a threat to society. Him and the girl both."

"How's this supposed to help me find him?"

"There's a woman," Dick said. "Her name's Charlotte Gardner. She's taken up with them. You find her, you find them."

On his way out, Park stopped at prison services, took a look at Dick's approved visitor list. Found what he knew he'd find. Charlotte Gardner, approved visitor with regular visits to Dick that stopped suddenly two weeks ago. That was Dick's angle. Revenge on a woman. It made Park feel better. Made him feel like he could move ahead. Made him allow himself to feel the buzz.

Park kept the buzz under wraps. It was actionable intelligence. He knew the Steel's angle. Now he just had to figure out his own.

34

BOXER

—

FROGTOWN

He'd told the crazy whiteboy not to teach him how to play the game. He meant it. Boxer loved speed chess. He'd learned it on the inside. When the whiteboy leaned down in his ear, told him he'd kill anyone Boxer and La Eme wanted, that he'd gun down the president of the United States and die smiling if La Eme would take care of his daughter, Boxer's chess brain jumped around the board. It landed in Hangtree.

Hangtree, California. The high desert just north of the border. A legendary place. Meth lab fumes and mirage shimmers all blended together. The Sinaloa cartel used to move weight through Hangtree no problem. Then the bosses switched. A sheriff named Houser took the throne. Houser had whiteboy sympathies. He had his own ideas about law and order. He organized the meth cooks. He gave them a patch of the desert. An old army base, nothing left but concrete slabs in the desert. The cooks set up. Houser became meth baron of the desert. He ripped off any cartel loads he could find. Him and his deputy. Legend had it Jimmy liked to snatch drugs and experiment on the carnales who passed through the local lockups. The ones lucky enough to live told about crazy drug cocktails Jimmy would cook up. Said he had mind-control theories and nutbag eyes.

Mostly Houser just robbed them and let them go. After all, he had a badge. The badge made him bulletproof. He let most of the cartel runners go. But not all of them. Boxer knew Houser dumped their bodies in the desert. Coyotes around Hangtree learned the taste of long pig. They got fat on La Eme flesh. They cracked teeth on buckshot hidden in the meat.

La Eme wanted Houser dead. La Eme knew killing a white cop in the desert could destroy them. Brown killers taking down an American cop, hell, it could lead all the way to military interdiction. Seal Team 6 cruising down to Sinaloa. And Houser knew it. He was bulletproof. He was fucking fearless.

A few months back Houser had grabbed a mule named Luis. Somebody found his body in the desert. He'd been gutted. They'd cut him open just to get out the balloons in his stomach.

Luis was Boxer's cousin. When they found him outside Hangtree, Boxer got mad. He had cop-killer daydreams. Then he thought it through. He played the chess game out. He lost every time. La Eme would never sanction a hit on a white cop. He learned to live with the idea that some folk were untouchable.

Then the crazy whiteboy dropped in his lap. A whiteboy willing to do anything. And then that little badass girl had shown him her wounds, and it had reopened the wounds inside Boxer, and he thought *why the hell not?* Fuck that the-cop-is-untouchable shit. No one's untouchable. If JFK can get got, the whiteboy could take out one lousy dirty cop. The *white* in *whiteboy* was key. If it went bad, nobody would blame La Eme. They'd put it on whiteboy insanity. Even if they took him alive, he'd never get a chance to talk. The Steel would have him dead in hours.

Boxer makes some calls. Coded messages spelled out the plan to El Presidente in Pelican Bay. El Presidente sees Boxer's logic. He likes the way it keeps their hands clean. El Presidente says greenlight on the high-desert cop. Send the crazy whiteboy. Killing Aryan Steel's president will be bad for business, at least short-term. But they only have to pay the price if the whiteboy lives. If he dies, they don't pay. Crazy Craig lives and the greenlight on the girl continues. Boxer doesn't like it. But he sees it's a pure business call.

Boxer calls in the crazy whiteboy for another meeting. Boxer meets him alone this time. He gives him the decision. He's going to assassinate a cop in the middle of the cop's own dirty kingdom. Boxer has to hand it to the crazy whiteboy. He keeps his face calm. Boxer can only see the fear in the whiteboy's throat, how it jerks and pops.

The crazy whiteboy isn't that crazy. He knows there's no coming back from a cop killing. He knows the price he's paying. His eyes a little too shiny, a little too wet. His voice comes out strong. No cracks in it.

The crazy whiteboy says, "I'll do it."

35

NATE

—

KOREATOWN / NORTH HOLLYWOOD

One last night. It's all Nate could ask for. Just let it be good.

Polly didn't know he'd seen Boxer. Didn't know the price he'd agreed to pay. Charlotte didn't know what he had to ask of her. Neither of them knew he was leaving tonight.

He took them all out to eat Korean barbecue. They dug the grill at the center of the table, where the strips of meat sizzled. They wrapped the charred meat in lettuce leaves. They didn't dig kimchi. Polly poked at it with a chopstick. She sniffed it. She said *no thanks*. She ate meat. She dipped her lettuce wraps in hot sauce. She laughed, her chin shiny with grease.

Charlotte laughed. She rubbed his leg under the table. She smiled. She leaned over and whispered, "This is nice."

If Nate could freeze life he would have done it just then. But of course he couldn't.

Later, long after Polly had gone to a meat-drugged sleep, Nate breathed in the scent from the sweat-soaked hair at the back of

Charlotte's head as their two sweaty bodies pressed together, moving in their unspoken rhythm. He thought about how you could care for someone and still use them at the same time. Maybe that's the way it always was. And then she reached back and her nails clawed his neck and for a while he didn't think anything at all.

LATER, IN THE QUIET and the dark, Nate told her what he had to do. What she had to do. She didn't try to fight it. She leaned in to smell the sweat of him. Asked him when he was leaving.

"Tonight," he said. "Will you do it?"

She said, "I will."

THEY MOVED CAT-QUIET through the house. He packed his bag. He took a fistful of the cash. He left the rest for them. Charlotte kissed him deep.

Polly slept nose to nose with the bear. Nate stood in the shadows watching her sleep. Felt something like hooks in his flesh tearing out parts of him.

He climbed into the green monster and drove out toward the high desert.

PART III

ZOMBIE WALKING

—

THE HIGH DESERT

36

POLLY

I-10

This couldn't be Fontana, the place she'd lived her whole life. Only months gone and now, as the places of her girlhood buzzed past them on the I-10, it looked to Polly like the streets and houses had all been torn up and put back together not quite right. The streets a little too small, the houses with angles just a little wrong, the sky a weird smudged color.

Everyone she cared about gone.

She should have known he'd leave her. She had believed him because she was stupid. Who cared about IQs or book reading or anything. When it came down to it she was dumb dumb dumb. She'd believed they were a family.

Charlotte drove with her knuckles white on the steering wheel, chewing chunks of skin from around her nails the way Polly used to do. Driving so careful, glancing over at Polly, not meeting her eyes. She was still scared of Polly after what had happened today.

Good.

SHE'D BURST INTO CHARLOTTE'S ROOM an hour before, her heart so violent she could feel it in the roots of her teeth. Living things danced all over in her.

"Where'd he go?"

"Polly, listen, honey."

"His bag is gone," Polly said. "The guns are gone."

He left you alone, her brain teased. *Just like you knew he would.*

"He's doing this for you," Charlotte said.

"I knew you'd ruin it. I knew it." The wriggling things rolling up her throat with the words.

"We're going to wait for him."

"He needs me," Polly said. "He can't go alone. He can't."

"Well, he did."

The things wriggling inside Polly had to come out. She picked up the water glass from the bedstand. She pitched it against the wall. Plastic cracked. Water splashed. It wasn't enough. She grabbed the lamp next. Raised it over her head.

"Now wait a goddamn second," Charlotte said. She grabbed the other side of the lamp. "Your dad is out there risking his life for you and you're here and that's all it is, so will you just chill the fuck out?"

Polly let go of the lamp. She realized of all the nutso things she was smiling. Smiling so big the corners of her mouth ached.

"Out there where?" she asked.

"What?"

"Out there where?"

"I can't tell you."

"Where?"

"Out in the desert."

"We're going."

"Polly, no."

"You can't stop me," Polly said. "You can't and you know you can't. I won't stop. I won't. So you take me to him."

"Polly, you can't—"

Polly had screamed then. A noise of rage. A warrior noise. And then she watched Charlotte shrink. Somehow Polly was the older one now.

"Get your keys," Polly said. She felt scared and alone but also somehow clean. "I'll get the bear."

Charlotte got the keys. They were on their way ten minutes later. As they pulled away, Polly saw a man, handsome and Asian, walking toward the building. He looked familiar, but she couldn't quite place him before they drove down the road and he shrank out of sight.

37

NATE

—

HANGTREE / SLABTOWN

See Nate in the desert.

See the corpse of a meth cowboy, his head turned round the wrong way, tire tracks crushed across his chest. See torn fences and smashed skulls. See a man naked but for a plastic apron letting scrub tear the flesh of his ankles as he runs away from the madness. See a rolled-over pickup truck. And Nate on the floor of the desert, searching for his breath, staring up at a condor in a clear blue sky while Houser stands above him, reloading a strange little rifle.

See Nate's silent lips move. Read them.

Polly, I'm sorry.

NATE HAD DRIVEN through the night to make Hangtree by dawn. He found some little AM radio station, some never-ending rock jam. Songs about space voyages and electric vampires. All of it faraway fuzzy like the signal had bounced off the moon. It fit the alien twists of the Joshua trees that hunched black against the star-filled skies.

He drove down an empty highway that ran parallel to some tracks, long trains coming up out of Mexico full of goods running the other way. The land was flat, dotted with a little scrub and old houses. It rolled on forever in every direction.

Hangtree seemed irradiated. Across a field on the side road something burned, maybe a shack or an old mobile home. It threw up black smoke. The smoke was perfect black, like it came from something burning away in its entirety. Packs of feral Chihuahuas ran the streets. They had missing eyes and mange. They scrapped. They ate trash out of the gutters. They humped on the road and in the dead grass where sidewalks should have been. People on the street came in two modes, too fat or too thin. They looked like they had been through the same atomic blast as the town.

Nate ate breakfast at the diner on the edge of town. He chewed stale toast and made murder plans. Now that he was here he had an ugly problem to deal with. Out here country stretched forever. It was forty, fifty miles either way before he'd hit highway junctions in either direction. To kill a cop in Hangtree, he'd need an hour's head start on the getaway or they'd seal off the roads before he could reach safety.

Like you're ever getting out of here, the ghost of his brother said in his head. *You knew this was a one-way ticket when you bought the ride. An escape plan is a joke.* Nate thought about Polly and made one anyway.

He finished his breakfast. He left a hundred-dollar tip. At the register he picked up a candy bar and a bottle of water. What the hell, make it two candy bars. As far as last meals went, he'd heard of worse.

He drove out toward Slabtown. He used the map Charlotte had put together from what she'd heard about the place. He rolled through hills on a gravel road. He saw a tree filled with shoes against the pure blue sky that stood in as Slabtown's flag. He parked off the road. He walked up the hill and crouched down. He looked down on a half-dozen concrete slabs with trailers sitting on them. The residents had no problem advertising their insanity. A goat head pentagram had been painted on the desert floor. One lab, white vapors drifting from a chimney cut through the camper roof, marked the edges of its slab with totem poles of melted and charred doll heads. Broken glass shimmered like a dry river down one of the gulches. Broken-glass wind chimes hung from flagpoles clattered when the breezes came.

He watched the trailers long enough to pick out the signs of life. The camp seemed empty. Only the lab with the doll heads looked active. After a while a man came out, naked except for his plastic apron. The man sat down bare-assed on the desert gravel.

Nate sat on the crest of the hill with the sawed-off in his lap and thought about fate. About how it wasn't the hand of God or anything like it. It was just the things that got passed down to you, the blood and the things the blood carried in it. And Nate could blame the blood or he could blame himself, but it didn't matter either way. He had to murder this man, this stranger he'd never know, who'd come here riding his own river of blood, half swimming and half following the current best he could without drowning. Killing him would summon Houser out here to the far desert where Nate could murder him and maybe, just maybe, get away clean. Well, not clean. Never that again.

Polly, I'm sorry.

He went to the green monster. He popped the trunk. He loaded up the shotgun. He walked down the hill to Slabtown. He dodged fossilized dog turds. He waited for himself to slip into that other world. That world of slow time, of seeing everything. But it didn't come. Something wrong. He wanted to see clearly, but all he saw was Polly.

He kicked in the door to the lab. Empty, although he'd just seen the aproned man go inside. Nothing but a bare-bones cook operation.

He checked the back window. Saw the aproned man run bare-assed across the desert. He had a big head start. Like he'd known Nate was coming.

They'd known he was coming.

It's a trap.

Polly, I'm sorry.

Gravel roared out in front of the trailer. Nate moved to the front window. A cop car came from behind a hill on the far side of the encampment, a pink hairless cop behind the wheel. Two truckloads of Slabtown Aryan Steel cowboys with hunting rifles and handguns came behind it. Nate guessed they'd been deputized. Time didn't slow down. It sped up so the breath moved too slow in his lungs. He was drowning in the desert air.

A trap a trap a trap. The song sang too loud for any other thoughts. The cop car stopped in a dust plume. One truck parked. The second one moved around to flank him.

Nate shot the pistol dry. The trailer window puked glass. Windshields shattered. Cowboys dove for cover. The truck out front rolled forward like the driver panicked and pushed the gas. The truck slammed into the trailer. Nate's whole world shook. He went down on his ass. Bullets snapped over his head. Nate ditched the .38. He grabbed the shotgun and ran toward the back of the trailer. He went through the door feetfirst. He surfed it onto the ground outside. He fell. He landed in dead grass. He rolled. He bounced off a chain-link fence. He climbed it. He swung a leg over. The wire spine at the top of the fence drew a quick bright line of pain across his calf. He dropped to the other side. He ran full blast. Engine roars bounced off the hills. Tires growled through gravel. War whoops floated.

He tried to think his way out. He had to get to the green monster. He would have to drive it off-road into the desert.

Gunshot.

He fired back with the sawed-off. The blast of it knocked the sounds out of the world. Nothing but *hummmmmm.* He looked behind him. He saw cowboys sprinting. He saw the flanking truck roll around the side of the house heading his way. Gravel rolled in waves as the truck spun out. One of the cowboys fell out the back of the truck. He crunched headfirst. He did a severed-spine shimmy. Nate fired again. The truck swerved. It ran over the man they'd just dumped. The truck cracked into a big rock. Truck tires spun in the air. The cowboys in the back kept shooting. Death missed Nate by inches.

He ran into the desert behind the lab. He dodged cactuses. He climbed a hill. He crested it to find another cop car. Houser was waiting for him, a short black rifle in his hands. Nate lifted the shotgun. Houser was faster. The rifle coughed. Nate went down. He ate gravel. The nerves of his chest one bright red ball. He puked up all his air. His lungs seized up. He flopped onto his back. His fingers fumbled on his chest looking for the bullet hole. Nate held his fingers in front of his face. They came up clean. He couldn't find the bullet hole. He ordered his body to scramble to its feet. It didn't. Houser came into his view. The cop loaded another shot

into the rifle. Nate watched him. He tried to talk. His vocal cords
didn't work. His voice came out nothing but rasps. It didn't matter. What he was trying to say wasn't for the cop anyway. It was for
Polly. Houser raised the rifle to his shoulder. He pointed the rifle
at Nate's head point-blank.

Polly, I'm sorry.

Polly, I'm sorry.

Polly, I'm sor—

38

PARK

—

I-10

Park drove bullet fast down the highway. He called Houser's cell phone again. He steered with his knees. He drank coffee. He chewed gum.

Voice mail. Third time.

"Sheriff Houser, this is Detective Park out of Fontana PD again. Following up on my lead on Nate McClusky. Wondered if he and his daughter had been spotted out in your neck of the woods. Sure you're busy so I just decided to hop on the ten and come on over to Hangtree myself. Maybe you can take me by this Slabtown."

What he said on the sheriff's voice mail was a lie. He wasn't paying a courtesy visit. He was chasing a buzz as strong and pure as he'd felt since he'd missed Nate and Polly at the motel.

It had been days of pure police work since he'd left Lompoc. He'd run Charlotte Gardner. He'd gone by her place, learned no one had seen her in a week. He'd gotten her auto info from the

DMV. Charlotte made poor parking choices. She had parking tickets on the regular. She had a street cleaning ticket in North Hollywood. Park went to that block. It only took a couple hours of canvassing before he found a woman who recognized both Charlotte and Nate, knew where they were staying. Polly she wasn't sure about. She said there was a girl, but not the one from Park's photo. A girl with bright red hair.

He called in an assist from L.A. County deputies. He ran a records search to find the house's landlord. He got verbal permission to go in. Inside he found clothes for all three of them. He found open drawers like they'd packed in a hurry. He found a glass of water with slivers of ice still floating in it. He'd missed them again, by hours this time. Park got mad. He kicked over a trash can. Wadded up papers rolled out. He unwadded one. A hand-drawn map of a town called Hangtree. A hand-drawn map of a place called Slabtown. As lab techs scoured the house for other clues, he'd talked to Sheriff Houser. He'd given the sheriff the lowdown on Nate McClusky. How he might be with a little girl. How he'd been robbing Aryan Steel spots. That he'd hit banks and storehouses. It looked like he was heading someplace called Slabtown. Looked like there were labs there. The sheriff said he'd look into it. That had been yesterday.

Park waited overnight out of professional courtesy. Then he hit the road to Hangtree.

Minutes after his last voice mail, his phone vibrated his nuts. He keyed it on.

"Park here."

"Detective Park, this is Sheriff Houser." His voice echoed, faint, like he was calling from deep under the earth.

"Been trying to get a hold of you."

"Well, here I am."

"Any sign of McClusky?"

"No, sir. No sign of your fellow up here at all. I went poking around Slabtown, didn't see hide nor. Could might be you're chasing a ghost."

"Well, I'd like to come up and take a look myself," Park said.

"No need for that," Houser said. Weird—Houser's tone buzzed him. "I'll be sure to give you a holler if I hear anything."

"I'll be in Hangtree in a hour or so," Park said. Long beat of silence after that. More weird buzzes.

"Head to the station," Houser said. "Deputy Jim Callen will meet you there. Just ask for Jimmy."

"And he can take me to this Slabtown place?"

Pops and hisses. A sound like Houser had a chest cold. Deep wet coughs.

"You all right?" Park asked.

"Fine as May wine," Houser said.

"So your man will take me to Slabtown?" Park asked again.

"If that's how you want it," Houser said, then killed the call.

Park had that feeling again, like he was a bullet midflight. Like it was way past up to him where he went or what damage he'd do.

39

NATE

—

THE HIGH DESERT

Nate woke up choking. He coughed wet red phlegm into his hands. A never-ending bomb exploded in his skull. The world came back in pieces. He bounced in the backseat of a car. A cop car. Houser in the front seat talking. Saying, "Fine as May wine." Saying, "If that's how you want it."

He touched his cheek where Houser had shot him. A hard swollen pocket on his face. Houser had taken him with a non-lethal round. A rifle that shot bags of pellets that took you down but didn't break the skin. They had known he was coming. They wanted to take him alive. They wanted something from him.

That scared Nate. Scared him bad.

His eyes unblurred. He focused on the back of Houser's head as the sheriff dialed his phone.

"Jimmy . . . yeah. Taking our prize to the shack . . . he don't think I know he's listening. Bet he's got a headache, though. Listen, it's that chink cop. The one who tipped us that our prize was

coming to town. He's on his way down here. He wants to see Slabtown . . . an hour, he said. I told him to find you . . . Think I don't
know that? There ain't no way to clean it up in time. There's shit
there no one can see, Jimmy . . . well then, that's just what you'll
do . . . just do it. No time for your experiments. Use one of Mc-
Clusky's guns. Leave the chink out in the desert. Call me when
it's done."

Plain talk.

That scared Nate most of all.

The car rolled to a stop.

Nate blinked. He sat up. He saw a shack with a dog guarding
it, something bred to guard the gates of hell. Nate saw the shack
and knew it was the place he would die. No way Houser would
talk so plainly in front of him. He'd kept Nate alive for some reason. Once the reason was gone, Nate would be gone too. And Nate
bet by the time death came he'd be glad to meet it.

40

POLLY

—

SLABTOWN

Venus had come to Earth and brought its storms with it. Slab-town looked like a spilled toy box. A truck sat crashed into the front of a trailer. Wisps of smoke curled up from the smashed trailer. Bullet holes pocked its face. Red stains on the gravel in front of it. A lump that used to be a man.

Out in the desert past the trailer, a man wearing an apron, his bare butt hanging out behind it, dug a hole. Another dead man lying next to him.

Polly looked at all the craziness and she knew it had come from her dad. She knew she was breathing in air he'd breathed not long before. And she knew that something had gone wrong. That if her dad wasn't dead now he would be soon.

I won't let it happen. I won't I won't I won't.

"Polly," Charlotte said. She put a hand on Polly. Polly imagined breaking her fingers. She put that thought in her eyes when she looked at Charlotte. Charlotte pulled her hand away like Polly was boiling. Maybe she was.

"Polly, listen," Charlotte said. "I know how to talk to these people. I'll talk to that man out there. He'll tell me what happened. Just sit here and let me talk to him."

"Find out where he is," Polly said. "Find out if he's okay."

The car started cooking in the desert heat the second Charlotte's door shut. Polly let herself sweat. She breathed in and out three times the way her dad had taught her. She tried to keep her mind on the flow of the air, how she felt it the most in the bend behind her nose where the air headed south to her lungs. She felt it in her belly swelling against her shirt. She didn't let any more thoughts come. The bear and she locked eyes until time went away.

Charlotte's door swung open. The hot desert air felt cool against Polly's skin as it rushed in.

"There's a shack up in the hills," Charlotte said. "They've got him. Some kind of rotten cops."

"He's alive?"

"Yes," Charlotte said. But her face said something different, something like *but probably not for long.*

41

PARK

—

HANGTREE / THE HIGH DESERT

The coffee the cop gave him tasted like cowshit. Park drank it anyway. The deputy, the one named Jimmy, gave him a grin like there was a joke Park didn't get. Jimmy drove fast and sloppy with that cop carelessness for yellow lights and speed limits. Hangtree was a true shithole, but something about it glittered as the sun came down. Something about the way the light flickered against the window glass made Park's eyeballs tickle.

"Sure you want to go out to Slabtown?" Jimmy asked. Park fought the urge to tell the man he was the color of a shaved dog. The thought made weird laughter inside him. He tamped it down.

"I told you already, Deputy, you don't have to come with me." The coffee at the bottom of the cup was gritty. He choked it down. Jimmy smiled so wide Park started to wonder if the fucker had spat in it.

They hit a dirt road that took them up a hill. Halfway up it Jimmy took a right into a wash that barely even qualified as a road. Park had been in a car all day. His kidneys were jammed to shit.

"I thought Slabtown was in an old army base."

"It is."

"This doesn't feel like the road to an army base."

"We're taking the back way in," Jimmy said. His eyes seemed like they'd migrated to the sides of his head. The fat fucker looked more piglike than ever. When Jimmy moved his head it seemed to Park that some of the molecules in the fat man's face moved slower than the rest.

Something was wrong. Not just with the situation, or with this dipshit townie cop. There was something wrong all the way down to the electrons.

Park tried to remember the last time he'd slept. How much caffeine he was running on. Tried to find some explanation for the body-thick vibrations echoing through him. His stomach roiled with them.

"Stop the car," Park said. Jimmy smiled that secret-joke smile again. His tongue flickered behind his teeth, a wet snake. Park locked his throat to keep from puking right then.

"Feeling poorly?" Jimmy stopped the car. Park undid his safety belt, ran out into the night, dropped to his knees, and puked into the rocks. He sat back on his ass and felt the world barrel roll. The sky above him was a smear of stars. They flickered; they danced.

Jimmy came up behind him. Too close. He had a sour smell to him like kimchi. Jimmy said, "I better take that." He took Park's gun with one hand.

"What's happening?"

"Ever hear of MK-Ultra?"

Park tried to make those words make sense. They didn't make sense.

"You put something in my coffee."

"You know that psilocybin mushroom? I grabbed some off a hippie a little while back. The CIA thought they could use shit like that for mind control. I like to run my own experiments. And you're a pain-in-the-balls chink who asks too many questions. So here we are."

The way his face throbbed to the beat of his words told Park this was no lie. Mushroom vibrations and adrenaline buzz all over him. *You are going to die* thoughts ricocheted all through his brainpan. But the animal panic was only a few inches deep. Something heavy and swelling sat underneath it.

"They say you see colors and shit," Jimmy said. "What do you see?"

"You're the color of a shaved dog," Park told Jimmy. Park laughed, and then he laughed at the laugh. The sound of it unwound within him. Like pulling a thread, threatening to turn him into a pile of string.

"Shit," Jimmy said. "You're totally fucking worthless. No wonder the CIA gave up on this shit."

Park dropped to his back. The earth was so cold under him. He looked up to the shimmying sky. He felt his skin against the air and knew there were no barriers, none at all, between anything. Him and the sky and all of it were just one big ocean.

Jimmy's pig-eyed face floated into his sight. He squinted at Park, like Park was out of focus—and maybe he was—and then Jimmy pulled his pistol from its holster and pointed it at Park's face.

This was the moment he'd been chasing. The buzz had led him here. It hadn't been the case or saving the girl that had driven him here. He'd been chasing death his whole life, he saw it so clean and clear, and now it was here and he surrendered to it in the moment.

Everything calm.

Okay then. Time to die.

Then an *oh shit* look washed over Jimmy's face like a wave. He put the gun back in its holster.

"Got to use the peckerwood's gun," he said as he walked away. Park tilted his head to watch him walk to his car and pop the trunk.

Park sat up. Tried to make sense of this moment he wasn't supposed to have. Looked down on the ground behind him to see if he'd find his body splattered under him. But no, he was still flesh. And he figured if he'd managed to be okay with dying then there wasn't anything that could stop him anymore.

He saw the rock next to his hand. Volcanic. Shard-shaped. Sharp.

He saw how it would fit into Jimmy just so. Like it belonged to him.

Park got the rock in his hands. He crouched down and moved toward Jimmy. Jimmy turned with a sawed-off in his hands. He looked right over Park's head as Park moved in.

Park brought the rock down. It fit into Jimmy's knee just the way Park knew it would. The fat man went down.

The desert rippled when Park ran. Like he was a giant and his feet shook the world. He ran into the scrub. Jimmy shouted all sorts of mad shit behind him. Jimmy swore he'd shoot. Jimmy shot. When the pellets whipped past Park he could see the paths they tore through the air. He ran after them. He chased those pellets out into the night.

42

NATE

—

THE SHACK

Dust motes swirled in sunset-orange light through the shack's window as the sun dropped all but out of sight. Nate watched shapes form in floating dust. A bird, a flower, a bear. He tried not to think about what was coming.

"I know who you are," Houser said as he tied Nate to a chair. It was hell-hot inside the shack. Houser sweated. Nate didn't. He figured his body didn't have any more moisture to give. The dust motes congealed into a solid image. Nick's face floated behind Houser. He nodded at Nate like *I'm here* and then the dust motes continued their dance and he disappeared.

"You're Nate McClusky," Houser said. "The scourge of Aryan Steel. Like something out of a country song. That's how they talk about you. You and your girl both."

"Keep her out your mouth." The ghost of his brother gave him an *atta boy*.

"You know as well as me you're going to die right here," Houser said. "You know you're going to die tonight. I won't do you the disrespect of trying to tell you any different. Only two things you got any chance of changing is just how easy that dying is, and what I do after."

"Okay," Nate said.

"You believe me."

"Pretty much."

"You're the one who took down the stash house in Sun Valley. You and your little girl."

"So?"

"So I know what gets sent down there. So I did some back-of-the-envelope figuring on it. The way I see it, a smart man could have cleared six figures off that caper. And it's not your only job. Someplace out there, you've got stashed either a lump of cash or a lump of that powder. Tell me where it is."

"We dumped it."

"Think I'm dumb?"

"We dumped the powder. All of it."

"You threw away a hundred grand worth of crank?"

"Didn't need it."

"You understand I'm going to hurt you."

He showed him a knife curved like a fishhook. Nate couldn't answer. He couldn't trust his voice.

Goddamn, Nick, I'm so scared.

Only way out is through, little brother.

"Maybe you won't believe me, son, but I don't want to do this. I don't like hurting a man. Not like Jimmy does. He comes back here before you talk, you'll see a man who takes pleasure in his work."

He's going to hurt me, Nick.

Yes he is.

"We flushed it."

"I'll believe it when I hear it from your girl's mouth. Maybe you tell me where she is instead."

Nate shook his head like *no.*

"All right then. Have it your way."

Only way out is through.

Houser started cutting. What followed made Nate understand how shallow he'd lived his life. It made him see that there was a deep core to him that he'd never reached, not in joy or sorrow, not in love or laughter. He found some final deep protoplasm at the heart of him that could only be reached with a knife.

He came out the other side of the cutting not sure what was him and what was the night. Sweat and blood slicked him. Houser wiped blood off the blade.

"Your money or your daughter. You're going to tell me, hoss."

Rope bit into Nate's wrists when he twisted them.

"Fuck you," Nate said. Or was it Nick?

"This ain't no song, boy. Tell me what I want to know and I can end this."

"Not today, not ever."

Stabs like puffs of wind. Drips. Houser breathing faster now. Working hard.

A slice. Something falling in a flap against his face. Nate reached out for the ghost of his brother in his head. But he was gone now. At the end of it Nate was alone. Nothing at all in the universe but this shack, this knife. The man cutting him.

Something urgent happened to his head. A great seal broken inside him. And the words wanted to spill out whatever hole had been dug in him. It wasn't the ghost of his brother or an outlaw code that kept him silent. It was deeper than that. That deep protoplasm knew one more thing than just pain. It knew Polly, and it kept her safe.

The digging ended. Nate floated. His vision was blurred, flat. New shadows darkened the room.

"Jimmy," Houser said into his phone.

"Yeah," he said.

"What?" he said.

"Where?" he said.

"Goddamn you," he said.

"Keep him in the desert," he said.

"You stupid son of a bitch," he said.

"I'll find him," he said.

Through the fog, Houser's shape framed itself against bright light. Houser had opened the door. Then he closed it. Houser was gone. The pain stayed.

43

POLLY

—

THE SHACK

They drove up the hill in the dark, moonlight showing them the rough outline of the pebble road as it curved up the hill. The shack stood against the sky a dark block. Above it, Venus blinked.

My home planet.

He was inside that shack. Polly knew it. She hopped out of the car before Charlotte had rolled to a stop. She clutched the bear against herself as she jumped from the car.

I'm from Venus.

"Jesus, Polly—"

She walked toward the gate. A thick chain snaked through it. She felt like she could snap it in two with Venusian hands.

She got close. A shadow broke itself from the dark and moved to meet her. She jumped back as the shape hit the fence. It made sounds like broken jagged things. It had yellow teeth and a death stench. The dog got its paws in the chain-link and stood face-to-face with her. It dropped ropes of drool. It had scars across its nose. It had death in its eyes.

"Oh shit," Charlotte said behind Polly. Polly ignored her. She'd done her part. It was up to Polly now.

I'm from Venus.

Polly took three deep breaths. She looked past the monster. She saw the rope at the side of the shack. On the third out breath she looked to Charlotte.

"We're going to get him," Polly said.

"Polly, that dog—"

"There's a rope to tie him up," Polly said. "On the side of the shed, see?"

Charlotte looked at her like *what?*

"I'm going over the fence," Polly said.

"That's crazy."

"When the dog's tied up, you climb in after me," Polly said.

"Polly, no—"

Polly climbed the fence, the bear in her hands. The dog growled, rocks smashing together in his chest. He snapped at her toes as they poked through the chain. He bit down. He tore the rubber toe of her sneaker. She felt hot wet breath through her sock. Saber teeth raked her foot. Red streaks of pain inside her. She yanked. Her foot popped out of her shoe. The dog yanked the shoe through the fence. He death-shook it.

"Polly, be careful," Charlotte said. Polly thought maybe it was the dumbest thing she'd ever heard anybody say.

She swung one leg over the top of the fence. The dog was done killing her shoe and stood below her. Ropes of wetness slopped down his face, staining his chest. He snapped at her. His face was full of scars. His eyes were full of death. She had time to feel bad for the dog. She wondered who'd hurt him so bad to make him this way. She wondered who had turned him into a monster.

She held the bear in her hands. He looked up at her face. He put his paws together and bowed to her like a warrior. She bowed back best she could.

"I love you," she told him.

Polly tossed the bear into the yard, just over the dog's head. The dog went for it. The dog latched onto the bear. It did the neck-snap shake. It pinned the bear against the ground and ripped. Stuffing flew.

I'm from Venus.

Polly jumped off the top of the fence. She hit the dirt hard. She bounced off the ground. She jumped on the dog's back before it could turn to face her. It bucked underneath her, fur-covered muscle so much stronger than her own. She lost her grip. The dog spun to face her. Polly scrambled fast. She hopped back to the dog's back. She wrapped her legs around its seething stomach and locked them together to hold herself there.

She pushed her left arm under the dog's neck. The dog scrambled underneath her. She knew if she let go she would fall, and she knew that if she fell she'd never get back up. She shifted her weight to stay behind it. The dog snapped the air inches from her face. Teeth crunched together, promised to tear her skin. The smell of rot filled her nose. She got her arm all the way under the neck, just the way her dad had taught her. Her hand found her other bicep. She locked in the choke.

She squeezed.

The dog growled, deep throat sounds that vibrated her choking arm. The dog's claws scraped dirt. The back claws tore into her legs. Bright pain flashes made Polly's eyes tear up. The dog tried to twist under her. If it could turn to face her it would have her throat in its jaws. They would shred her easy as they shredded the air. She pressed her body down, her forearm up. She hugged the throat with her whole body, the way her dad had taught her.

She squeezed.

The dog's neck was so thick. She pressed with everything she had. The dog's legs buckled. The growls turned to wheezes. Her arm muscles burned. Threatened to rebel. She knew she didn't have much left.

She squeezed.

The dog went out all at once. It went limp, dropping them both into the gravel. Polly let loose. She knew the second she let go blood would rush to the dog's brain. She stood. The world did a quick pirouette. She got steady. She got out the rope from the side of the shed, looped it through the collar, tied it to the fence. The dog snorted. She didn't have long. She tied the rope to the fence. She didn't rush it. She did it right.

When she was done tying up the dog, she picked up the bear from off the ground. He was split open along the stomach. Blue-and-white stuffing leaked out of the hole. She fell butt-first on the ground and hugged the bear, rocking him, rocking herself.

"So brave," she told the bear. "You were so brave."

44

CHARLOTTE

—

THE SHACK

Charlotte hopped the fence while Polly rocked herself on the ground out of the dog's reach. The dog shook its head, clearing cobwebs. Polly looked up at her. The thing behind the girl's eyes made Charlotte gasp out loud.

The reality of what she'd just seen, what the girl had done, came to her in one rush. It was the craziest thing Charlotte had ever seen in her goddamn life. She laughed like glass shattering. Polly looked up at her like Charlotte was the crazy one. Maybe she was.

"Is he okay?" Polly asked. "Somebody hurt him to make him that way. It's not his fault."

Polly handed the remains of the bear to Charlotte. Charlotte realized she could feel her tongue drying in the night air. Her mouth had been hanging open ever since Polly jumped into the yard. Polly picked a rock up off the ground. She raised it over her head to smash the doorknob.

"Polly," Charlotte said. Polly stopped with the rock over her head.

"Maybe try it first," Charlotte said.

Polly turned the doorknob. The door swung open. Polly tossed the rock, headed inside.

A sour-sweet smell hung in the air, a smell Charlotte knew from her uncle's shack in deer season. It was the smell of blood both new and old. Polly pushed ahead. She stood in the doorway.

"Nick?" It was Nate's voice. It was the voice of an old man. "Nick, I didn't say a thing. I didn't."

Polly ran to him. Charlotte followed.

They'd tied him to a chair with rough twine. Purple wet furrows in his wrists where he'd fought against the rope, rubbed his skin away. Pinkflesh dots all over Charlotte knew to be cigarette burns. Blood on his chest, a bib of it from his mouth, from his face. Stab wounds in his chest weeping something darker than blood.

Polly held him fierce.

"It's not Uncle Nick," Polly said. "It's me. I found you and you can't leave ever again. You can't."

"We've got to untie him," Charlotte said.

He heard Charlotte, lifted his head slow up at her. Her brain needed a second to identify the wrongness, the one blue gunfighter eye staring at her, the dark red pit staring at her.

Oh god they took his eye.

45

PARK

—

THE HIGH DESERT

The desert seems silent until you are being hunted. The night seems dark until you want not to be seen. Park hunched to the earth, zigzagged through the scrub. The night had brought a million million stars stretched out overhead to the edges of everything. Below, rock and cactus stretched out to the same forever.

Staring up at the ululating sky, Park tripped over a rock. He went facedown. He slid down a hill. A cactus broke his fall. Pain pricks from spines all over. Holes in his skin, air on his inner flesh.

He didn't know why he was being hunted. Why the deputy had fed him the mushrooms. It didn't matter why. Only that it was happening. He understood that he was nothing but vibrations like the scientists said. He managed to wrest himself away from those thoughts, to focus on where he was.

He'd hurt the fat deputy's leg. He doubted the man could follow him into the desert. That meant Park was safe for the moment.

He needed to get his bearings, look for the glitter of Hangtree. He climbed a ridge. He reached the top of a rock. He reached up for the moon but he couldn't quite touch it. He turned in a slow circle until he found the lights of the town.

A bullet snapped past his ear. It left a bright red line in the night.

He left his body long enough to see himself at the top of the ridge, painted against the sky. He'd made himself a target. And they'd found him.

Gunshot.

A little star was born and died in a valley below him. The gunman moved from the shadows, surefooted through the scrub. It wasn't the fat deputy hunting him now. Park guessed it was Houser. The man moved toward him, fearless, knowing Park wasn't armed.

Park moved down the other side of the hill. Something slashed at his leg, yanked him down to the desert floor. He reached down, felt cold metal. Barbed wire strands from a long-dead fence. He yanked at it to clear it from his leg. The strand ran about a yard long.

Rocks hissed on the slope above him.

It was Houser moving. Park moved too. He'd passed through something now. Now he felt no buzz, no thing at all. He wasn't even sure he was a thing. All the walls between him and the world were just ideas, and he was just an idea, and when he died the idea was the only thing that would cease and every volt of energy and every molecule of him would stay, so who could say that death was a thing?

Yet he planned to not die.

Park felt the cold of the desert leach into him. He drank up the desert cold. Cold all the way through. A lizard walked across his foot. Like a message from the world telling him it was true. Park was a lizard, cold all the way to the blood, just exactly as cold as the world around him. We're all lizards that way, he thought.

He was a part of the desert now. Houser moved down the hill. He moved sure-footed but uncertain. He stumbled, a stranger in his own desert. Park moved behind him, moving so slow, so silent. Houser's animal instincts must have kicked up, something from the base of the brain honed by millions of years of eluding the wolves, that told him to spin, to raise his gun. Park's hand came up, knocked the pistol off course. The gunshot as Houser pulled the trigger flashed and boomed and wiped away the world for both of them.

They fought then on the desert floor, both blind and deaf. They stumbled and fell on each other. Park felt Houser's hands on his skull. His head slammed into the dirt. Flashes of color burst through the blindness. He felt a pool of nothingness open up around him. He bucked with all his strength, felt Houser lose his balance on top of him. Park wormed his way backward. Sharp pain snagged in his back. The barbed wire. He reached behind him and yanked the strand out from under him. It tore furrows in him but he got it free, just as sight and sound started to return around the edges of existence, just as Houser scrambled onto him once again.

Houser got his hands on his skull again. Park got the loop of wire around the sheriff's head. He yanked both hands so the loop tightened on Houser's neck. Blood squirted hot against his skin. Houser poured all over him. He squealed and splashed. Park made noises too. He shared the man's death with him. He watched the soul flutter out of the man. He saw his last breath like a white puff of smoke. He heard the ghost fly by. When it was done he left the body for the desert to take.

HE SAW A SHACK on the top of a nearby hill. He moved toward it. He found a road that led to the shack. He stepped onto the road. The night caught fire, lit from the path below, twin headlights blinding him. The car door opened. The fat deputy came out, shotgun raised, all of him a streak against the night to Park's eyes.

"Where's the sheriff?" Jimmy asked.

"Everywhere," Park said. He wore a bib of blood, black in the moonlight, still warm from Houser's body. "He's right here for sure."

"You bugfuck motherfucker," Jimmy said. He raised the shotgun. Park walked down the hill toward Jimmy. The barrel of the gun was a swimming hole. He was ready to dive in. His feet shuffled in the dirt. Everything music. Everything strings.

"Ain't no way you could have killed him," Jimmy said.

"Weird, right?" Park laughed. The air he sucked in tickled his lungs.

Jimmy kicked Park down at the side of the road. He stepped back into the road and raised the shotgun. He had a smile on his face. Park smiled back. He meant it. He opened his arms up into the night. He felt every grain of oxygen in the air, the warmth of every pinprick of light from dead stars overhead. He wondered if he would feel the buckshot pass into him, join him, and separate him. He hoped so.

A hiss like sudden rain came through the night.

They both turned to face the thing rolling down the hill. A car rolling with no headlights. The car hit Jimmy head-on. It knocked him into the air. He came back down headfirst. His body twisted on itself in a way that a body can't do. The brake lights of the rolling car glowed red. Dust kicked up as the car slid to a stop.

Charlotte Gardner sat behind the wheel. Polly McClusky sat

shotgun. She had the face of someone twice her age. She had a gun pointed at Park. Park still had his arms in the air from seconds before, when it had been the deputy who had the gun on him. One gunman traded for another. So goddamn funny he had to laugh.

"Polly?"

She looked at him. Emotions like roiling fish on her face.

"You're the guy," she said, her voice so different from when they'd spoken on the phone. "The to-help guy. Why are you here?"

"I'm here to help," he said. He walked forward. He saw Polly held her bear in her lap, its stomach split open.

"Oh no," he said.

A weird frog croak came up from the backseat of the car. Polly tilted her head toward the shape.

"He wants to talk to you."

"The frog?"

"Huh?"

"Nothing."

Park walked to the back of the car. The backseat was gore. Nate McClusky's life was spread out all over the seat. It glowed with it. Nate McClusky was cut up, oozing, one eye sliced out.

Nate took him in with his one eye.

"You get him?" Nate asked. "The sheriff?"

Park nodded *yes* before he could even start to figure out if it was a thing he should admit to.

"You put it on me," Nate said.

"What?"

"Killing the sheriff. You pin that on me."

Nate lay back with a smile on his face. It occurred to Park that he was supposed to arrest Nate now, but it was just a thought and he paid no mind to it.

"We've got to go," Polly said to Charlotte.

"Are you going to be okay?" Polly asked Park.

"Yeah," he said. "Thanks for asking."

"We got to get him to a hospital," Polly said. "Thank you for looking for me. You don't have to anymore."

HE WATCHED THEM head down the road into Hangtree. Then they were gone and Park was alone in the desert. And he stood there next to the cop car. He took off his bloody shirt and he realized he was cold and he climbed in the deputy's car and he drove away.

PART IV

PERDIDO

—

CALIFORNIA

46

POLLY

—

BIG BEAR

It hurt her to look at him. Real pain at the center of her chest. Her heartbeat sounded like *save him save him save him save him.*

He had refused a hospital. He'd told Charlotte to drive them someplace safe, a place to hide. She'd steered them into the mountains, to a place called Big Bear. Evergreens like wooden fortress walls stood on either side of the road. Cold mountain air made Polly shiver. They found a cheapo resort with cabins in the woods. They moved her dad in under cover of darkness, Charlotte and Polly on either side of him to keep him upright. Little noises forced themselves out of his mouth as he moved. She knew how little he wanted her to hear them, so she pretended that she didn't.

Charlotte went out to find food. Polly washed her dad's wounds. She was a good nurse. She'd done it before.

"It's over," she said, rubbing salve on a cut across his chest. "We can take you to a hospital."

"Not yet. If I get caught now, I'll be dead soon. That Boxer fellow seemed all right, but maybe not the type to pay a debt to a dead man. I have to stay hidden until Craig Hollington is dead."

"Please," Polly said. "Please. I don't want you to die."

"Just take care of me," he said. "You're the best at it."

"And then can we go to Perdido?"

"And then Perdido."

THEY LIVED OFF white-bread cheese sandwiches and gas station tamales. There was a computer at the lodge. Charlotte went there every day to check the news. Polly's dad was front page for a while. There was a manhunt. Detective Park was declared a hero. Nate McClusky was a cop killer on the loose. Park did them a favor and didn't mention Charlotte.

Polly cleaned her dad's wounds and cut his food. She stuffed cotton in the hole where his eye used to be. He said it didn't hurt. He was lying, but that was okay.

When it was just the two of them, her dad would talk and talk. Stories she'd never heard before, stories about their family. He told her about his brother Nick, and how he could ride a motorcycle on one wheel, and how he'd knocked out a man in the cage in eight seconds. She told him about fighting the dog, and he clapped his hands, and he took her face in his rough hands and said he was proud, and his one eye watered and then her eyes did too.

They told stories about Perdido. What they would do there. How Polly would turn brown in the sun. How her dad would become a great fisherman. How the bear would learn to surf.

Her dad grew scar tissue. But not all the wounds closed. He burned to the touch. Charlotte bought him two canes so he could walk to the bathroom on his own. Once Polly saw him there, sitting down to pee with his shirt lifted. She saw the stab wounds, how black they were, and she had to look away to stop from going crazy.

Charlotte sewed up the bear. Polly gave him to her dad, who needed him more than she did. The bear and he convalesced together. He learned to work the bear's movements almost as good as Polly. He held the bear in his hands and made him move. He put the bear's mouth to his bottle of water and had him drink. The bear's paws flew to his crotch like *I got to pee*. Her dad stuck his finger between the bear's legs so it stuck out the front and had the bear joyfully take a leak off the side of the bed. Polly's cheeks went red and she laughed until the muscles of her stomach were weak and shaking. He laughed too, even though the laughing tore things open again.

She could feel the fever in him, his body still fighting. Hot purple streaks on the skin around the wound.

Polly woke one night. She saw Charlotte mopping her dad's brow.

"It's getting worse," Charlotte said.

"I'm not going anyplace until the deal's done."

Charlotte made a sound, not with her mouth, just her throat. Polly watched her wipe her face.

A few days later Polly sat watching him sleep when Charlotte came through the door.

"He's dead," Charlotte said. "They got him."

The news had just broken. A maximum security murder in Pelican Bay. Blades tied to broom handles had speared Crazy Craig dead in his cell. He bled out overnight. A massive lockdown, statewide, to prevent chaos.

Her dad smiled. He hadn't been sleeping after all. He opened his one good eye and took Polly's hand in his and said, "Just one more thing to do. I got to sit down with them."

"Why?" Polly had a crazy thought that she could swallow him to keep him safe, that it was the only way to do it.

"To let them know I'm still out here. Still dangerous."

"No," Polly said. "You can't. You're hurt too bad."

"It's got to be done," he said. "So I'm going to do it. After everything you did to save me, you got to let me do this little thing. This last thing."

"Then Perdido," she said.

"Then Perdido."

47

POLLY

—

BIG BEAR / CASTAIC

She'd thought she knew what strong meant. She'd thought he'd shown her already. But she had been wrong.

He got out of the bed with the help of the two canes. Charlotte and Polly helped him shower. His body was muscle and scars, red veins lacing through his skin. He got dressed. He put their last pistol in the back of his pants. He moved so slow. They put on his drugstore eye patch. They loaded up the car. Nate shambled to the car like a grandpa. He fell into the backseat, breathing hard, wet with sweat.

Polly climbed into the backseat with him. Charlotte drove down the hills once more, back toward Los Angeles.

When they got close to Castaic, the place of the meet, Charlotte pulled over at a rest stop so Nate could change his shirt. The one he had been wearing was spotted with soaks of blood. He wouldn't let Polly look at him while he changed shirts. She turned her back to him. She looked at the reflection of him in the car window. All the cuts all over him just looked like gutters dug into him.

They'll see how weak he is. They'll see it and they'll fight us and we'll lose.

The meeting was in a truck stop diner. It wasn't the truck stop Polly and Nate stopped at that forever ago, but it was close enough that it felt familiar to Polly.

Charlotte parked in the back.

"I'll get the canes," she said as she put the car in park.

"No canes," he said. "I'm walking in."

"I'll help you then," Charlotte said.

"They see you helping me, we're all dead."

"Jesus pete, you can't—"

He lifted a hand like *be quiet.*

"They can't know how hurt I am," he said.

"They'll take one look at you and know."

"You think I don't know that?"

"So let me—"

"Polly comes with me. You stay here."

POLLY CAME OUT FIRST. She moved around to his door. She watched him breathe in through the nose, out through the mouth. He opened his eye. He stood up holding the car. Little muscles in his face twitched. He smoothed them out. He took deep breaths. His shoulders came up. His face cleared the pain. He looked as strong as he had in front of her school, a million years ago. He smiled at her and she couldn't see anything behind the smile but strength. He tucked his pistol into the front of his pants.

"Bring the bear," he said. "He's good for us."

They walked into the truck stop together. The bear dangled in

Polly's hand. Her dad rested his hand on her shoulder, not for support, but somehow the other way, like he had so much strength to spare that he could pass it on to her.

He walked into the restaurant strong and sure. Polly followed him. The sounds of the world seemed so loud to her now. Their feet, the hum of people throughout the diner talking. The world more real than real. Polly followed him to a back table where two men sat, one Hispanic and one white. BROWN PRIDE on one's bicep, WHITE POWER across the other's throat.

"You sit down first," he whispered to her as they got closer to the table. She scooted in across from the two men. Nate scooted in next to her. She knew the cuts on his stomach must burn with the motion. He didn't give it away.

The one with the Brown Pride tattoo started to talk. Her dad cut him off by putting his pistol on the table and covering it with the newspaper.

"The deal was no weapons," the white one said.

"But you've got one anyway," her dad said. "I'm just being upfront with you. Now let's get down to business."

The Brown Pride guy talked first. He said that Crazy Craig was dead. Somebody named Moonie was running things for Aryan Steel on the inside now, and that's the way it was going to stay. Polly repeated names to herself, so she'd remember them if her dad wanted to talk about it later. Brown Pride said Aryan Steel had agreed to lift the greenlight on Nate and Polly.

Her dad nodded like *good*.

"Let me see the kite," he said.

The White Power guy passed a handwritten note across the table to her dad. He glanced at it and then pushed it over to Polly.

"Read it," he said, then turned to the other men. "My eyes ain't quite what they used to be."

To all the solid soldiers on the block
Or in the street
The greenlight on Nate McClusky is lifted
The greenlight on Polly McClusky is lifted
There will be no payback
There will be no retribution
On penalty of death
There will be peace
Steel Forever, Forever Steel
Moonie, president

When she was done reading, he nodded like *good*. He smiled big and broad. Polly wondered where he'd put his pain. Where he'd put his weakness.

"We're going down to Mexico," he told the men. "At least until the heat dies down. But before I go, I need you to hear one thing. Polly might come back from Mexico before I do. And if a hair gets harmed on my daughter's head, well, then, I'll just find my way back from Perdido. Y'all won't see me coming. You understand what I'm saying?"

The White Power one looked at her dad like he was the monster under the bed.

"Moonie's spread the word," he said. His tough guy mask wasn't very good. Polly wondered if he hadn't been enough places yet. She figured hers was better. "The greenlight's lifted. We're cool."

Her dad picked up the newspaper with the pistol under it.

"Then we're through here. Polly."

He touched her on the shoulder. His hand felt like he'd run it under the cold tap. She kept the shock of it off her face. They walked out of the restaurant without looking back.

On the way back to the car he threw away the newspaper into

a trash can. It thunked loud. *Too loud,* Polly thought. They were halfway to the car before she realized what it was. He'd thrown away his gun.

HE CLIMBED INTO THE BACKSEAT. He sat up strong. He patted the seat next to him.

"Want you on my good eye's side," he said.

She climbed in next to him.

"We good?" Charlotte asked.

"We good," he said. "Let's go."

Polly watched the traffic behind them as Charlotte steered them back toward L.A.

"I don't think there's anybody," Polly said. The bear shook his head like *me either.*

"I think you're right," he said. "I think we're home clear."

And before she could even agree he tilted over like a statue being pulled down.

"Daddy—"

"The glass feels good on my face is all. I need a rest."

He reached over to her without lifting his head. He squeezed her arm.

"Will they do what they say?" she asked.

"It's not what they said that matters. But the fear's worth plenty. The fear on that whiteboy's face. I just wanted to look into a face and make sure it was fear I saw. And that's what I saw. It's over."

They crested the San Fernando Mountains so that the bowl of Los Angeles hung beneath them. The sun set behind it. The tall buildings of downtown were backlit with impossible colors, pinks and oranges and reds. The sky behind Los Angeles burned.

"Wow," Polly said.

"I've lived all over," Charlotte said. "You can't beat Southern California for sunsets."

"It's 'cause we're so dirty," Polly said.

"How's that?"

"Dirty air," she said. "Light bouncing off the trash in the air, it splits up the light. Makes it pretty."

"It's a hell of a thing," her dad said. But Polly saw his eye was closed.

As they rolled down the mountain it felt to Polly like the car fell toward L.A., coming down smooth, like how she imagined flying must go, as the dirty skies burned beautiful and faded to purple and black.

They were back from the skies and on the streets of Hollywood before she tried to wake her dad up.

48

PARK

—

STOCKTON

He'd known where Polly was for a while—when she'd surfaced in Stockton, it had made the news, of course, and if he'd still been on the force he would have been one of the battalion of cops who interviewed her. But he didn't go. Not for the month he spent on medical leave, or the six months after that he took to get himself out of the police force with a good chunk of his pension.

All told it was a year after that desert night when he'd driven up to Stockton. He'd gone to her cousin's house first, a beer-fat man who gave Park a mean look that he dropped as soon as he understood who Park was. He remembered him from the news stories, and he told Park where to find her. Park could see on the man's face that he was scared of something, and that something kept Polly treated right.

Park drove to the strip mall the cousin sent him to, found the martial arts studio, and walked into a kids' grappling class. He joined the parents watching from the side of the mat. On the mat pairs of kids in T-shirts and shorts wrestled. Their sweat dripped. No sounds but scuffles, grunts, gasps, the occasional slam. The teacher, a wiry young man with a Brazilian accent, coached kids from one corner. Park looked over to a line of duffel bags resting against one of the walls. A familiar brown head poked out from one of them.

Polly's cherry hair, same as it had been in the desert, made her easy to find. She'd grown three inches. She'd gotten ropy. She wrestled with a bigger boy who wore a boy's downy mustache. She got the boy's back. She scrambled for the choke. The boy muscled out of it, turned around so he was the one on top. He tried to twist an arm behind her back. The boy, stronger, pushed her arm higher, but she fought it off. She didn't win but she didn't lose either. The coach blew his whistle. The fight ended. Polly and the boy slapped hands. She laughed. Her eyes were so blue. Not like a lake. Like rivers.

The coach called for a break. Polly moved to the side of the mat and scrubbed her face with a towel to sop up sweat. Park walked to her. She saw him from the side of her eyes. She turned to him quick. Her animal instincts were fine-tuned.

"Hey," she said. Waiting for him to make the move.

"You have a home," he said. "How is it? Everything okay?"

"It'll do," she said. "It sort of has to, you know?"

"What about Charlotte?"

"Still in L.A.," she said. "She offered, like we could stay together, but she didn't mean it. I could tell. It's okay."

"What about your dad?"

"He went down south," she said. "To Perdido. He can't ever quit hiding. He's a cop killer, right?" Her eyes said *we have a secret.*

"Yeah," Park said. "But from what I hear he isn't hiding. From what I hear he's down in L.A."

She smiled like *oh yeah?*

"I heard your dad ripped off an NDP drug house in Santa Cruz last month. I got that from two different friends in the department."

"Huh."

"So did he?"

"If they said he did, he did."

"But you said he was down in Perdido."

"So then that's where he is."

"They found the body of a man named Aaron Carter. Goes by the name A-Rod. From what I've put together, you two had a couple run-ins with him. A bad hombre. They found his body a week ago. He didn't die good. Word on the Aryan Steel grapevine was it was your dad who did it."

She looked at him like *so what?*

"But you know what I think?" he asked.

She shrugged like *tell me.*

"I think Nate's dead."

"You just said he killed a guy. How'd he do that if he's dead?"

"I think he's dead. I think he's just the rumor now. Like Robin Hood or the Boogie Man. A legend."

She didn't say anything. He nodded to one of the gym bags against the wall. The bear's head poked out of it.

"I see he pulled through."

"It's the best part of not being real," she said. "It means he can't die."

Park didn't ask who she was talking about.

"And you're safe?" he asked her instead.

"As long as Dad's alive and people are scared of him, I'm safe. And he's alive. So I'm safe."

"What if they find him, Polly?"

Her tough-girl face broke a little. In the face underneath he could see shovels, hard earth, a long night for Polly and Charlotte.

"Yeah," he said. "Right."

The silence thickened between them.

"Maybe I can help you," Park said. "Get you into a good school. Get you headed toward a normal life."

She smiled like she was the adult and he was the kid.

"Normal life? I don't get to have one of those. But I get to have something else. That's okay. I never was normal anyway. I'm from Venus."

"What?"

"Never mind."

The coach blew a whistle.

"I got to go," she said.

"Right," he said. He fumbled for words. He didn't know why he'd come all this way. Just to see her? Make sure he hadn't imagined all that in the desert?

She turned back to him.

"Hey. Thanks for looking for me. It made me feel good that someone cared."

"I didn't care," he said. "Not when I hunted you. I did it for my own reasons. But I do now."

"Weird," she said. "Later."

He watched her for a while. Watched her roll on the mat, watched her fight and lose, fight and win.

"Cooldown," the coach said. Polly and the other kids started stretching, shaking the fight out of their system, drinking water. The parents stood.

As Park headed for the door, someone started some music, something with bass in it, something wild and alive and free. Park didn't know what it was called, but he thought it suited the girl just fine.

ACKNOWLEDGMENTS

Novels are hard. First novels are harder. Thanks to everyone who put up with me as I struggled to yank the damn thing from my skull.

Thanks to Jedidiah Ayres and J. David Osborne for early reads and input. Thanks as always to Nat Sobel and Megan Lynch for their support and acumen. Thanks to Boards of Canada, Electric Wizard, Sunn O))), Sleep, and Earth for the writing music.

Thanks to the bear, who isn't real, but is true.

ABOUT THE AUTHOR

Jordan Harper is the author of *Love and Other Wounds*. He has been a music journalist, film critic, and TV writer. Born and educated in Missouri, he now lives in Los Angeles.